What Readers Are Saying about For~~bidden~~

"Nothing I have seen provides bett~~er spiritual~~
equipment for today's youth to figh~~t and win the~~
spiritual battle raging around them than Bill
Myers's Forbidden Doors series. E~~very~~
family should have th~~ese~~

C. Pet~~er~~
Preside~~nt~~

"During the past 18 y~~ears~~
have been involved in ~~have seen~~
a definite need for the~~se. Bill fills the need~~
with comedy, romance, action, and riveting
suspense with clear teaching. It's a nonstop

The Forbidden Doors Series

FORBIDDEN ● DOORS

the cards

BOB DEMOSS

Based on the Forbidden Doors series created by Bill Myers

Tyndale House Publishers, Inc.   Wheaton, Illinois

Visit the exciting Web site for kids at www.cool2read.com
and the Forbidden Doors Web site at
www.forbiddendoors.com

Published in association with the literary agency of Alive
Communications, Inc., 7680 Goddard Street, Suite 200,
Colorado Springs, CO 80920.

Scripture quotations are taken from the *Holy Bible,* New
Living Translation, copyright © 1996. Used by permission of
Tyndale House Publishers, Inc., Wheaton, Illinois 60189. All
rights reserved.

This novel is a work of fiction. Names, characters, places,
and incidents are either the product of the author's
imagination or are used fictitiously. Any resemblance to
actual events, locales, organizations, or persons, living or
dead, is entirely coincidental and beyond the intent of either
the author or publisher.

ISBN 0-8423-7185-0, mass paper

Printed in the United States of America

07 06 05 04
5   4   3   2

To Gretchen Hansen,
fifteen years and still
a faithful friend

Then we will no longer be like children, forever changing our minds about what we believe because someone has told us something different or because someone has cleverly lied to us and made the lie sound like the truth. Instead, we will hold to the truth in love, becoming more and more in every way like Christ, who is the head of his body, the church.

Ephesians 4:14-15

1

*P*hilip reached between the folds of his mattress and retrieved the knife. He pulled it from its sheath and stared at its nine inches of cold, hardened steel. A thread of the November moonlight danced along the edge of the blade as if fearful of being slashed. Philip clutched the handle. The sweat in the palm of his hand almost caused him to lose his grip.

His tired eyes scanned the darkness around him and settled on the digital clock. With a squint, he noticed it was 2:27 A.M. Sleep had escaped him all night. He figured his bed must look as if it had been dumped into a blender. Hours of tossing and turning had created a jumbled maze of sheets and blankets.

Philip slumped to the floor and leaned back against his bed, careful not to accidentally slice himself.

At least not yet.

The knife had been a gift from his dad several months after his mother split with his two sisters. Dad had promised they'd go hunting. Although that was years ago, at times the memories were still as fresh as the tears on his face.

Of course, they never went hunting. *Big surprise there,* Philip thought, placing the knife on the carpet next to him. He drew his legs up to his chest. His dad made lots of promises he never seemed to keep. Philip figured the knife and the promised hunting trip was just his dad's way of trying to smooth things over—or was it to buy his loyalty?

According to the judge during the divorce proceedings, once Philip turned eighteen, which he did next month, he could choose to live with either parent. Some choice. An oppressive dad or a mother who walked out on them in the middle of the night.

Philip missed his mom, no question. But he hated her for leaving, not that he completely blamed her. All his parents ever did was fight. If it wasn't one thing, it was another. When his dad got drunk, yelled, and threw things, that was the last straw. Mom was gone before the sun rose the next morning.

Even now, the memories flooded his mind with a fresh dose of pain. Why did life have to be so hard? The darkness of his room seemed to close in on him. He reached around and squeezed the base of his neck, which ached as if jammed into a vise. If only he could silence the voices in his head. Then maybe, just maybe, he'd find the peace that eluded him.

Sitting in the dark, tears staining his face, he wondered what the kids at school would think about Mr. Self-Confidence now. After all, most of his friends thought he had it all together. He had a cool car. His dad made tons of cash. They lived in a big house. And, when it came to clothes, he could buy whatever he wanted. No wonder his friends always came to him with *their* problems.

But where could he go with his?

If only his friends knew how close to the edge he had drifted. Sure, part of him wanted to show everyone he had it all together. He wasn't looking to blame someone else for the fact that he wore a mask. Like his dad, he didn't let anyone get too close. How many times had he heard his dad say, "Don't show them you've got issues, buddy boy. It's a sign of weakness."

But the game of being perfect was getting old.

He was tired of the charade.

He was tired of squirreling away his problems.

To make things worse, he couldn't take another day of fighting with his dad about where to go to college next year. Philip's dad wanted him to go to the same university that he had attended. Like father, like son. When the letters of acceptance from several big colleges came in yesterday morning, his dad had thundered, "Son, if you're smart, you'll go where I went."

Philip peered at the knife and his heart started to race.

Was this the way out? Would this silence the pain?

Why not put it all behind him right here, right now?

What if he did? Would he be missed? Would anybody really care? Sure, his girlfriend Krissi would be a basket case for a week. But she'd get over it once she found another popular senior to hang out with, right? Philip caught himself. *Why am I being so cynical about her?* Krissi, he knew, cared for him deeply. They had been together for years. She was the best friend he ever had. Why, then, did he write her off so quickly? Maybe he *was* losing his mind.

So why not end it all?

He reached for the knife and balanced it in his right hand. His lungs tightened as he considered the finality of this action. Maybe if the future was bright, maybe if he knew for certain it would be worth living, maybe then he'd reconsider. But, as far as he could see, nothing added up. His thoughts turned to Krissi. Even if things worked out between them and they got married someday, would she, like his mom, leave him at the first sign of trouble? Probably. So what was the point of pressing on?

He swallowed hard.

A new, more disturbing thought jolted him like a bolt of lightning. What if Scott and Becka were right about God? What if, as they claimed, there really was a God, a heaven, and a hell? What if those who didn't believe in him would spend forever burning in hell? Worse, what if Scott and Becka were right and there wasn't any way to change his mind?

He lowered the blade. Philip knew he

wasn't ready for that final encounter with God—*if* there was a God.

Exhausted, he reached for the remote and flicked on the television. Maybe the drone from the box would help him numb the pain—or at least help him sleep. The TV, another gift from his dad, was complete with cable and sat on the hamper that he never used. The TV jumped to life with such brilliance, he had to slam his eyes shut until they could adjust to the light.

As his eyes blinked into focus, a woman, wearing a turban and sitting at a table, filled the screen.

Philip inched up the volume.

". . . we all possess this inner wisdom. The cards are just the gateway to the supernatural. They allow us to tap into our inner selves and can give us answers to life's most troubling questions."

Philip leaned forward. At the bottom of the screen he saw her name listed as Madame Theo, Psychic, Advisor, and Spiritual Counselor.

"Tonight, whether you're young or old, I know you have questions. I know you have problems. Don't be afraid to connect with the cosmic reality to find your personal answers."

Philip suppressed a laugh. *What a joke,* he thought. *As if Madame Theo knows squat.*

"Give the tarot a chance," she said. Her voice was as smooth as silk and as warm as the afternoon sun. The camera zoomed into her wrinkled face. "Yes, I have been used to help police solve crimes . . . loved ones to find each other . . . young people to find the right college—"

That got Philip's attention.

"And tonight," Madame Theo said as the camera zoomed in for a tighter shot, "I promise I can help you discover your destiny."

Philip tilted his head to the side. Several thoughts nagged at him. What if she's right? He had read somewhere about people who were missing who were found because of someone like Madame Theo. If she can help the police, maybe she's on to something, right? What harm could there be to check it out? On the other hand, he vaguely recalled a special on TV exposing psychic fraud. Maybe this lady was different.

"I'm so convinced that the tarot is a gift to us from the other side, I'll personally give you a free reading. Just call the toll-free number on the bottom of your screen . . ."

Before he knew what he was doing, Philip reached over to his nightstand, tore a scrap of paper from a textbook, and jotted down the number and address of Madame Theo's Palace. He snapped off the TV and, in the darkness, decided to return the knife to its hiding place.

For now.

～

"That's a wrap," a voice announced through the overhead monitor.

Madame Theo lingered at the desk where she had just finished another live, thirty-minute local broadcast. Her eyes, black as raisins, scanned the tiny setup. It wasn't much, just a desk, a chair, a dozen candles and, behind her, a backdrop of the city of Crescent Bay, California. But it was a start. After a month of broadcasting three nights a week, she noticed a significant jump in business.

She gathered her tarot cards, tucked them into an oversize handbag, and then eased out of her chair. At sixty-seven, she projected the air of a trustworthy grandmother, at least that's what Fred Stoner, her producer and chief financial backer, had said. She suppressed a sly smile at that memory. She circled around to the front of the desk and walked past two cameras mounted on tripods, careful not to trip on the thick cables that covered the floor like snakes. She headed for the exit.

Fred Stoner bounded through the door, almost bowling her over. "Big news!"

Madame Theo steadied herself and met his eyes, expectant.

Fred tucked a clipboard under his arm. "Listen, the station loves what you're doing."

She smiled faintly. "I'm gratified to hear that, Fred."

"You should be," he said, picking a piece of lint off the lapel of his navy blue suit coat. A patch of black hair poked out the front of his white shirt, unbuttoned at the collar. "You've made a huge sacrifice doing the graveyard shift."

She nodded. "It's been hard. You know I'm not a night owl."

He took her by the arm and led her to the hallway. "Here's the deal. They want to move your program to the 10 P.M. slot."

"Really?"

"I knew you'd be happy about that," Fred said. He smiled wide, revealing his perfectly straight pearly white teeth. "There's more."

She raised an eyebrow. It almost collided with her turban.

"We're talking syndication, Madame Theo."

"Oh, my," she said, pretending to be surprised. She adjusted the handbag strap on her shoulder. "The cards said this would happen." That was an understatement and she knew it. Indeed, just the day before, while seeking wisdom from the cards, she experienced one of the more dramatic encounters with the spirit world. She'd keep that bit of information to herself. After all, Fred, she knew, wasn't a true believer in the divine forces at work. He was Mr. Businessman. Which was okay. One day he might come around to her way of thinking.

"I'm sure they did," he said with a slight smirk. "Anyway, if everything goes as planned, we're talking every major city up and down the California coast. The sky's the limit from there."

Madame Theo slipped her arm out of his and turned to face him. A worried, almost tormented look crossed her face.

"What is it?" Fred asked, appearing crest-fallen.

She bit her bottom lip for a second before answering. "That means we'll be seen in Los Angeles, too, right?"

"You bet," he said, rubbing his hands together as if in anticipation of a juicy steak. "Hey, it's only the largest market in the country."

She looked away. During yesterday's encounter, her new spirit manifestation never impressed upon her there would be such obstacles. Then again, direct contact with the spirit world was a whole new dimension for her. There was so much she didn't understand. If only she knew how to pro-

ceed. During her next contact she'd make
a point to gain clarity.

Fred took her by the arm and, with a gentle yet firm tug, turned her back toward him.
"What aren't you telling me?"

Madame Theo's eyes blazed with energy.
"I think . . . well, that a show in Los Angeles
might be a problem."

"Because?"

Her eyes narrowed. She lowered her voice
a notch. "I can't tell you, at least not yet."

2

*P*hilip bent over
and plucked a pair of jeans and a T-shirt
from his *almost dirty* pile on the floor, which
meant he had worn the clothes at least once,
maybe twice. With a quick sniff he figured
they'd be good for another day.

He jerked the shirt over his head, jumped
into the pants, and then rushed down the
stairs, pausing for a split second to steal a

look in the hallway mirror. He ran his fingers through his dark hair and noticed his blood-shot eyes looked battered. The nasty head-ache thumping between his temples didn't help matters.

He darted into the kitchen and flung open the cabinets, hoping to grab something quick. It was Monday morning and he wanted to cruise by Madame Theo's store to check things out. He knew the only way to squeeze that in before school was if he could escape before his dad cornered him. On the second shelf he spied an opened box of Pop-Tarts. Perfect.

"Oh, good, you're up," his dad said, coming into the kitchen from behind him.

Philip's heart sank. He snatched the Pop-Tarts, turned, and careful to avoid eye contact, muttered, "Um, hi, Dad."

"You're not going to school like that, are you?" he asked, adjusting his tie around his neck.

Philip's head pounded at the question. "Dad, since when did you become the clothes police?"

"Ah, watch it there, buddy boy," his dad said with a slight edge in his voice. "I guess you know your shirt looks like a wrinkled prune."

"It's the new style," Philip said with a little more sarcasm than he actually felt.

"When we were kids," his dad said, taking a step forward, "I'll have you know we had to wear a uniform to school. And our shoes had to be polished."

"Dad, that was before the flood."

"What's eating you?"

"Nothing," Philip said. He tossed the box of fruit-filled, rectangular, perfectly manufactured nutrition on the table. He spun around to face the refrigerator, yanked open the door, and strangled a bottle of milk. With a sharp twist, he wrenched off the lid, grabbed a glass from the counter, slopped the milk into the glass and, in his hurry, onto the counter.

"Oh, that's just great, buddy boy," his dad said, fastening his belt around his waist.

"Sorry—"

"What am I, the maid?"

"Dad, I *said* I'm sorry. I'll clean it up."

His father walked to the coffeemaker and reached for the coffeepot and started to pour a cup. He cleared his throat. "Tell me, Philip, what are your thoughts about college?"

Philip spoke with his mouth full. "Dad, don't go there. I don't have time to—"

"We're talking about your future, son," he said, pouring a cup of coffee. "Now listen. I spoke with the dean of students at the University of Berkeley and they—"

Philip cut him off. "Can't this wait?"

"I'm not just saying this because you're my son," he said, ignoring the remark. "But a kid like you, with your grades, can write your own ticket. I realize in many ways you're a lot like me. You're tall. You're handsome. You've got brains. And you especially want to keep your options open. I don't blame you for that."

Philip blew an impatient breath.

"Still, I know you'll love Berkeley, son." He took a sip of his coffee. "What I can't figure is what you have against it."

With each passing second, Philip felt hopelessly trapped in a conversation he didn't want to have, certainly not now. Couldn't his dad understand that maybe, just maybe, he wanted to go somewhere else? Somewhere where the teachers wouldn't be asking, "So you must be the son of blah blah blah." The jackhammers drilling between his temples didn't help. He wolfed down the rest of his Pop-Tart, spied the clock on the microwave, then stood to leave.

His dad looked up over the edge of his coffee cup. "You didn't answer my question. Where are you going, anyway?"

"School, remember?"

"This early? You don't usually leave until—"

"Dad, please, give me a break here. I've got stuff to do."

"Let me guess . . . you're giving Krissi a ride," his dad said, placing the cup on the table in front of himself. "She can take the bus, son. This is important—"

Philip almost snapped. "Dad, this has *nothing* to do with her."

"Then why can't you stay and talk for a few minutes? I thought you'd be interested to know what the dean said."

Philip snatched a paper towel and wiped up the spilled milk. "We'll talk later, I promise." Philip ducked out of the kitchen before his dad could say another word.

Upstairs, he grabbed his books, his car keys, and then snatched the paper where he had jotted down the address and number last night. He stuffed the note into his front pocket before racing out of the house.

Once outside, he jumped into his convertible and closed the door with a wham! If he hurried, he'd still have time to cruise by Madame Theo's Palace.

Maybe she could help him make sense of his life.

Maybe the cards would reveal where he should go to college.

Maybe they'd give him a reason to keep living with a hyper-controlling dad whose hyper-expectations of his brainy son were stifling.

Maybe.

Philip hesitated, putting the car in reverse as a new series of thoughts engaged his mind. He didn't know the first thing about tarot cards, telling the future, or Madame Theo, aside from what he saw last night. *Is this crazy or what?* he thought. *What if she's just another quack?* There was only one way to know for sure: he'd check her out for himself. Maybe good news awaited him in the cards.

If not . . . well, he refused to think of the alternative.

～

Scott Williams worked his way through the lunch line, loading his plate with Monday's mystery meat, Tater Tots, creamed corn, a carton of milk, and a sickly cup of Jell-O 'd Crème, which was basically a square of red Jell-O with Cool Whip and a fancy name. He handed the cashier his student lunch card and then headed into the main dining area.

"Hey, Scott," Krissi said, batting her perfect, killer eyelashes. "Becka's got our seats saved . . . over there." She nodded toward the back wall.

"Cool. Be right there," Scott said, scoping out the room.

When Scott and his sister, Becka, first started attending Crescent Bay High, after years of being away on the mission field in

South America, he definitely had to learn about the seating dynamics in the cafeteria. Everybody had their place. True, the pecking order wasn't written down anywhere official. But anybody with half a brain couldn't miss it.

Many of the freshmen sat closest to the ice-cream bar.

The nerd types next to them.

The upperclass jocks hassled anyone who dared to approach their table by the windows. The coolest jock, of course, sat at the end. While the cheerleaders were an exception (they could approach the jocks without being tackled), cheerleaders usually filled a table of their own.

The corner opposite from the jocks was home to the druggies and fringe kids, and those who wore black everything. The honor students and those in chess club or on the student council took the center two tables. And, while the most popular kids sat wherever they wanted, they usually picked a table by the far wall.

He started to walk in that direction.

The seniors, he noticed, always parked their trays on the table nearest to the faculty lounge as if to imply they would be next in charge if the faculty decided not to show up one day. Scott sat down next to his sister.

"So, Becka," Krissi said. She placed her tray on the table and then removed the items, one by one, organizing them into positions as if setting the table for the queen of Sheba. "Did you see Philip today?"

"Yeah, for something like a half second," Becka said. "He looked pretty, um . . ." She paused, as if to think of a kind word.

Scott butt in. "Just say it. He looked like he had a close encounter with a herd of cattle."

"Really?" Krissi flipped her auburn hair over her shoulder.

"Yeah," Becka said, nodding. "I can't say for sure, but I'd say he seemed really stressed, too."

Scott poked at his dessert. "His eyes were all puffy and red like this gross Jell-O."

Krissi appeared to be considering that. "I bet his dad's been riding him about college again," she said, placing her napkin on her lap.

"Could be," Becka said. "I don't know. I kind of think there's something else bugging him. So what about you guys? Is everything cool between you two?"

Krissi blushed. "Of course. We're doing great. I mean, sometimes . . . well, when we talk about the future, he, like, gets this faraway look in his eyes."

Scott tossed a Tater Tot in the air and scarfed it down. He swallowed. "Speaking of your man," Scott said a little too loudly, "there he is."

Krissi and Becka turned around as Philip approached their table. His hair looked as if it had been caught in a tornado. Shirt wrinkled. Eyes bloodshot. He plopped down next to Krissi without saying a word.

"Hey, there," Krissi said. "I missed you. You okay?"

"I'm fine." Philip started to shovel lunch into his mouth.

"Could have fooled me," Scott said with a cheesy grin.

Philip glared at him. "Who asked you?"

"Excu-u-use me for living," Scott said, raising both hands as if surrendering to the police.

Nobody spoke for a long minute. Becka swallowed a bite of lunch and said, "So, Philip, what's the latest on your college scholarship—"

He cut her off. "I really don't feel like talking about it."

Krissi and Becka exchanged a concerned look. Krissi turned to him, her eyes softened. "Are you sure you're okay?"

Philip didn't answer.

"I mean," Krissi said, putting her arm around the back of his chair, "you seem so tense—"

He brushed away her arm. "What's this? Pick on Philip day?"

Krissi pulled her arm back and dropped

her hands to her lap. "Nobody's picking on you, babe."

Scott wiped his mouth with the back of his hand. "I know. You're worried about the big debate tomorrow, right?" Scott, although two years younger than Philip, was on the debate team with him.

Philip's eyes reddened. "Wrong-o, Scott."

"Then what's up?" Becka said softly.

Without warning, Philip jumped to his feet. "Can't you guys take a hint? I don't feel like talking. And if you *must* know, I'm tired of everybody sticking their nose in my business."

A low whistle escaped Scott's lips. "Speaking of being tired, dude, maybe you should get some sleep, you know?"

Philip pointed a finger at Scott. "Don't start with me. You know, you're just like my dad . . . always telling me what to do with my life."

"Hey, it was a joke," Scott said, shocked by his friend's overreaction. "I didn't mean to start World War III."

"Come on, guys, just give me some space," Philip said, then hustled out of the room.

~

"Mom, I'm telling you," Becka said that evening at the supper table, "I've just never seen Philip with such a short fuse."

Mrs. Williams dabbed at the corner of her mouth with a napkin. "In what way?"

"Well, he's always been a really nice guy. And just about everyone at school likes him," Becka said. She was momentarily distracted as her dog Muttly started to beg for a treat. "No, Muttly, you've already had enough for one day." She scratched him behind the ears instead. "Anyway, he was really kind of abrupt with all of us at lunch. Not his usual self and all that."

"I'm sorry to hear that," her mom said. "What does Krissi think?"

Becka sighed. "She says Philip's dad is bearing down on him about college. Plus, there's a bunch of stuff going on between his parents. You remember they're divorced, right?"

Mrs. Williams nodded.

"Well, it has something to do with where Philip will live next month," Becka said. "Krissi thinks the pressure has been really getting him down."

"That's got to be tough," her mom said, reaching for her cup of coffee.

"News flash!" Scott said, barging into the kitchen.

Becka and her mom turned toward him.

"You've got to come and see this," Scott said, beckoning with a wave of his hand.

"See what?" Becka asked.

"I just got an e-mail from Z," Scott said, his

face glowing with excitement. "Something's up, big time."

Z was a buddy they had met in a chat room on the Internet. Z always seemed to have a mission for Scott and Becka to undertake, usually involving some level of spiritual warfare. But it had been several months since Z sent them on a new adventure.

"So tell me," Becka said, starting to get out of her chair. "What was his message?"

"You'll never believe it," Scott said. "Z sent a link to a psychic Web site and told me to download a video clip of some lady called Madame Theo."

"Really? Why?" Mrs. Williams asked.

"Z said we need to help a friend trust God for the future or something like that," Scott reported. "Who knows, maybe this person is mixed up with a fortune-teller. Does anybody come to mind?"

Becka walked over to Scott. "Well, Mom and I were just talking about Krissi and Philip's situation."

Scott looked puzzled. "You think the friend Z is talking about is Krissi?"

"Could be," Becka said. "Or Philip."

3

*M*adame Theo
sat alone in the near darkness at a small desk.
The desk, cluttered with assorted papers,
books on astrology, notes, and a receipt
book, was tucked away in the cramped back
room of Madame Theo's Palace, a ground-
floor, two-room storefront at the edge of
downtown Crescent Bay.

She folded her thin, bony fingers together

and rested them in her lap. Although it was three o'clock Monday afternoon, the drapes were drawn tight. She preferred candlelight to sunlight.

Her forehead was a wrinkled knot—not from age, but from the concern that had troubled her ever since Fred Stoner mentioned syndication into the Los Angeles market. While his excitement was unmistakable, he didn't know about her past. How could he? She had never told him about her years in Los Angeles.

It wasn't really any of his business, right?

Besides, that was decades ago.

When she agreed to work with Fred, she never guessed the past would come back to haunt her. Now, like a frightened cat, she found herself backed into a corner. Fred was a natural promoter. One of the best she'd ever seen. He wouldn't stop until Madame Theo was on national television.

How, then, could she insist she didn't want to be seen in Los Angeles? Fred was sharp. If she made up some phony reason, he'd press her until he knew the truth. That was the kind of guy he was. And, since the local television station was interested in syndication, she knew she'd have to confront the demons of her past sooner or later.

Unless she decided to drop the whole thing and not agree to the syndication. Of course, Fred would be furious. He'd say she could forget about her TV show. He'd say the station wanted ratings—especially with the revenue that ratings and syndication would bring.

Either she went all the way or not at all. She closed her eyes and whispered, "Spirits, speak to me as you did before. I'm listening. Is this the direction I should take?" She opened her eyes and followed the flame of a candle as it danced to the cadence of an unseen current of air. Watching the movement produced a trancelike state. In the tranquillity of the moment, a name from the past came to her mind. He was the one person who might know what to do—if she could reach him.

"Yes, thank you," she said, excited at the inspiration from the other side.

She reached down and opened the bottom desk drawer. Under a stack of papers, she found what she was looking for: a well-worn sheet of paper. Although it had yellowed around the edges with time, the list of phone numbers was still discernible. She laid the page on the desk and smoothed it out with the palms of her hands.

At the bottom of the page she spotted a handwritten name and number scribbled in pencil. At the sight of his name, a fount of memories gushed to mind. Had it really been thirty years since she had first jotted down his name? She picked up her phone and then dialed. What choice did she have?

She brought the receiver to her ear.

"Law offices of Jacobs, Barnes, and Zimmerman," the voice of a young woman announced after the second ring.

"Yes, I'm calling to speak with Zack Zimmerman."

"Who may I say is calling?"

Madame Theo hesitated. "Just tell him . . . an old friend."

"I'm sorry, ma'am," the receptionist said, her voice professional but clipped. "Mr. Zimmerman is very busy. Can I take a message?" As she spoke, Madame Theo heard the ring of other phones in the background.

"I . . . well, listen, can't you tell him it's urgent?"

"I'm sure it is," the receptionist said with a touch of contempt. "All of his calls are urgent. But if you won't give me a name, I can take a message—or put you through to his voice mail if you'd like."

Madame Theo considered that. She knew Zack's style. If she left him a message—voice or otherwise—he might not get it for days. High-profile defense attorneys were usually juggling more cases than they could handle. Zack was no different. He'd be swamped. But she needed him now, not in a week. She just had to speak with him directly.

Madame Theo took a long, slow, cleansing breath. "Okay, then, please tell him . . . Rita Thomas is calling."

"I'll see if he's available. Please hold."

Afraid she might drop the handset, Madame Theo squeezed the phone against the side of her head as tightly as her crooked fingers could handle. She was so focused on what she was about to say, she paid little attention to the nondescript sound of Muzak playing in the background.

Thirty seconds later, the familiar, thick voice of Zack Zimmerman filled the earpiece. "Rita? Is that *really* you? I thought you were dead."

~

Philip pulled his car to the curb, turned off the engine, and then sat for a long minute. Although he was as motionless as a mannequin, his heart raced to keep up with the questions flooding his mind. Was he really going to do this? What were the odds that a little stack of cards could give him the answers and the hope he craved?

What would his dad think?

Philip had parked under a tall oak tree several doors down and across the street from Madame Theo's Palace. From where he was positioned, he had a clear view of the front door and was surprised not to see anybody going in or coming out.

Maybe he needed an appointment.

Maybe she was closed on Mondays.

Maybe she was at a late lunch.

Maybe I should just leave and get my head examined, he thought. One thing was certain. No way did he want to be seen going inside by a friend, especially not Krissi. As much as he liked her, he knew Krissi sometimes had a tough time keeping her mouth shut. If word got around school that he went to have his cards read, his friends would dog him for days, maybe the rest of the year—if not his entire life.

After all, Philip was the brain of the bunch. Under most circumstances he relied on logic, on reason, and on his intellect to sort things out. How could he explain that he went to some palm-reading, fortune-telling, card-dealing woman for answers? Even *he* found that notion hard to believe. Then again, last night, this woman seemed so caring, so in touch with something she had called "the cosmic reality."

He had come this far, why not go for it?

He slipped on a pair of dark sunglasses.

With a squint, he read the sign on the door: Open. Walk-Ins Welcome. He checked his rearview mirror before cracking open the door. The coast was clear. It was now or never. With his heart in overdrive, he gulped a quick breath, jumped out, and then darted across the street.

His steps slowed as he approached the doorway. With a glance over his shoulder, he reached out, turned the knob, and slipped inside. As the door opened, a little cowbell sounded, announcing his arrival. He removed his sunglasses. It took a second for his eyes to adjust to the darkness.

As the room came into focus, he noticed it wasn't much bigger than his bedroom and was lit by candles mounted on metal stands. A card table and two chairs were in the middle. Thick, red curtains hung from the walls, and a velvet black cloth, like dark clouds, hovered overhead covering the ceiling. He felt as if he had stepped into another world.

He had hardly taken a step forward when the odor of strong, cinnamon incense filled his lungs. To his left, he observed the source: an incense pot puffing away. Directly across the room, he noticed an open doorway covered with strings of beads. He couldn't see beyond that to the next room.

Puzzled, he waited a moment. Now what?

As if in answer to his unspoken question, Madame Theo parted the beads and glided into the room. "Welcome," she said. With a wave of her hand, she motioned toward the chair closest to him. "Please have a seat. I can sense you are troubled in spirit."

Philip's heart jumped into his throat. How did she know that?

Catching himself from leaping to conclusions, he figured she probably said the same thing to everyone who came in. Why else would they be here if they weren't troubled? Most folks wouldn't come to her for a tea party, right?

"I . . . I saw you last night," Philip said, his voice almost breaking. "On TV, that is. I thought you might be able to help me with . . . um . . . the future and stuff." He pulled the chair out and sat down. His eyes darted around studying her every move.

Madame Theo smiled as she eased into the other chair. Her turban, like a massive bandage, was wrapped tightly around her head. She wore a floral-printed muumuu. The one-piece gown floated around her as she moved as if caught in a gentle breeze. She placed her hands on the edge of the table like a dealer at a casino waiting for the players to place a bet.

When she didn't immediately start to speak, Philip said, "This is the first time I—"

She brought a finger to her lips. "Please, not a word. Before we begin, I must focus on the energy you brought into the room."

Philip swallowed. Was she serious? What energy? He wasn't aware that he had brought anything with him besides his pounding heart. He crossed his arms and waited. The silence that followed was almost as thick as the incense.

After what felt like an eternity, she spoke. "Tell me your first name." She closed her eyes in anticipation.

"It's Philip."

She nodded as if he had uttered something profound. She opened her eyes and gave him a penetrating look. "I sense that you are impatient, Philip. Do you know anything about the gift of the tarot cards?"

He shook his head. "No, ma'am."

"But you believe in their power?"

"I . . . well, let's just say I'm open to learning more." No way would he let on about his skeptical nature. She had a lot to prove if she was going to sway his thinking.

Another nod. "It's a start," she said softly. "The tarot cards allow us to tap into the well of our inner wisdom."

"Cool." Philip forced a smile.

She raised an eyebrow. "It would be best if you didn't interrupt the process."

"Sorry." He dropped his hands into his lap.

"You must understand, Philip, that this is a sacred moment," she said, lowering her voice. "Tarot cards are not a game. They are connected to, and take us to, the cosmic treasury of knowledge passed down from before time itself."

Whatever that means, he thought but didn't say it.

"Each of us is on a journey," she said, placing the deck of cards in front of her. "Tarot cards reveal the energies and life forces which are in motion at the time we conduct a reading."

Philip nodded, as if this made sense to him.

Madame Theo laid a hand on top of the deck as if touching a holy relic. "There are seventy-eight tarot cards divided into three groups: the major arcana, of which there are twenty-two. You might look at them as trump cards."

Trump card. At last, something he understood.

"The minor arcana, with sixteen cards, appear much like the king, queen, knight, and page cards in a regular deck. The third grouping is the forty pip cards."

Philip watched as she shuffled the cards. For all he knew, the cards were marked.

"Let us begin," she said. "May the spirit guide move into position the order of the cards." Madame Theo placed the deck in the center of the table. She continued to speak after a brief pause. "There's one more thing, Philip, before we proceed further."

"Yeah?"

"Do you know what divination means?"

"You mean, as in the *occult*?" He hoped his voice didn't betray the panic he felt at the word. He had seen the effects of the occult before when Krissi fooled around with channeling and wanted nothing to do with it.

She nodded. "Again, I sense your apprehension. Please, Philip, the word only means 'hidden.' There is nothing to fear here. Tarot cards are a systematic form of divination that allow us to divine the future course of our lives. You do want to know about your life, don't you?"

He swallowed hard. Maybe yes, maybe no. Certainly not if he ended up possessed by some crazy spirit, thrashing around the room like Krissi. But Madame Theo said there was nothing to fear, so why not? He managed a nod.

"I will conduct a basic three-card spread this afternoon." She peeled off the top card, followed by the second and third cards, laying each in a row, faceup.

Philip leaned forward. As far as he could tell, the first card looked like a bunch of stars. The next card had a picture of people leaping from a building that had been struck by lightning. The image bothered him. He

felt the overwhelming impression to leave. At
the sight of the third card, a skeleton in a
suit of armor riding on a horse, a little voice
at the back of his mind told him to leave.

Madame Theo pointed a long, thin finger
at the first card. "This represents your immediate future," she said. Shifting her finger to
the second card, she said, "this points to your
near future. And this," she added, lowering
her voice just above a whisper, "represents
your distant future . . . unless circumstances
change."

Philip scratched the side of his head.
"So . . . what do they mean?"

The pupils of her eyes narrowed to the size
of a pea. "Let me just say I rarely see three
trump cards in a row. That means you are
a special person."

He liked the sound of that. Maybe there
was something in the cards for him after all.

"The first card," she said, resting a finger
on it, "is the star. Your star is on the rise. You
will be successful sometime very soon."

Philip smiled. "In the immediate future.
Cool."

"This second card is the tower," she said.
"Although it may appear frightening, it actually means in the near future you must make
some drastic changes."

"Like, what kind of change?"

"Maybe in a friendship or relationship or

situation." She leaned forward. "Does anything come to mind?"

Philip searched his thoughts. Maybe it meant he needed to break up with Krissi. Or maybe he needed to avoid Scott. Or perhaps he was supposed to move out of his house and away from his dad. He shrugged. "I guess there are several things I can think of."

Madame Theo brought a hand to her chin. "Don't jump to conclusions. Keep in touch with your inner voice. Allow the forces of the universe to speak to you. You'll know what to do at the right time."

"All right," Philip said, growing a little weirded out by the whole experience, yet somehow he was drawn to know more. "But what does this last card mean?"

Madame Theo hesitated. She adjusted her turban and then rested her hands in front of her. "That, Philip, is the death card."

His heart spiked.

She raised a finger. "I can tell by the look on your face that you are filled with fear."

Yeah, and I can hardly breathe, he thought. "What does—"

"Don't let it disturb you, son. While it may suggest that death awaits you in the distant future," she said, reaching across the table to touch the back of his hand, "it also points to the need for transformation."

Philip's heart almost exploded inside his chest. "But it *could* mean I'll die. . . ."

"Young man, just remember, the death card was dealt last. That's a good sign."

"How so?"

"Death is not, shall we say, inevitable. There's still time to change your course."

"But how?"

"By heeding the warning of the tower," she said, pointing to the center card with a single tap. "Change the relationships that are holding you back, that prevent you from growing. Then, and only then, will you avoid the consequences of the death card."

Philip wanted to run as fast as he could from this place, this woman, these cards, and that awful incense. He wanted to make whatever changes he needed to avoid the death sentence. For some reason, he couldn't move. He remained helplessly frozen in place. He felt as if an anchor had been tied around his waist and he had been tossed into the bottom of the sea.

4

"So where's your brother, Becka?" Ryan Riordan asked, tapping his ring against the steering wheel of his Mustang.

"I thought he'd be here by now. I wanted to see how they did in debate class." She scanned the parking lot, hoping for a glimpse of Scott.

They sat in Ryan's car parked against the

back wall of the school parking lot where the seniors always parked. Although the spaces weren't reserved for the seniors, the juniors knew better than to park there. It was just one of those unwritten rules of high school life.

"Nothing personal, but I've got stuff I've got to do on my project," he said, checking his watch. "I think the library closes early on Tuesday, right?"

"Yeah, I think so," Becka said, looking at her boyfriend. She could tell he wasn't upset, just pressured to get to work on his senior project. "I'll tell you what. I'll just catch up with Scott at home," Becka said, finding it hard to stop gazing into his eyes."

"In that case, I say we hit the road." Ryan reached over to the ignition and, with a wink, fired up the engine.

Ryan's thick, black hair framed his killer, sparkling blue eyes. As usual, Becka's heart skipped a beat when he smiled at her, that smile with the little upward curl at the corners.

No wonder Ryan was one of the most popular kids at school.

And, while she always found him attractive, she was at a complete loss as to what Ryan saw in her. Take Krissi. She could double as the Miss Perfect Barbie doll. Or Julie Mitchell, her best friend on the track team, with her beautiful blonde hair.

By comparison, Becka saw herself about as nondescript as a houseplant. What could be so attractive about her thin, mousy brown hair and equally thin, nearly nonexistent body?

Whatever his reason, Ryan seemed to enjoy her company. A lot.

And lately, Becka couldn't help but wonder what would happen next year after he left for college. Would they still keep in touch? Would they go deeper in their relationship even though they'd be apart? Like her mom always said, "Absence makes the heart grow fonder."

Or . . . to wander, Becka countered.

What if he met some college girl with a million talents, who'd found a cure for cancer and whose dad was a wealthy president of some big company? Becka was afraid he'd forget all the great times they had had together and be married to Miss Wonderful his first semester at college.

They drove a few minutes in silence. Ryan was the first to speak. "So what's on your mind?"

"Me?"

He flashed a grin. "Do you see anybody else in the car?"

Becka blushed. "I . . . I was just thinking . . ."

"About?" He turned the car toward the Sonic several blocks from school, a favorite new drive-in, burger-and-shake joint, where the waitresses skated to the car with your order. "I missed lunch. Thought we'd grab a shake."

Becka was glad for the distraction. "Sounds great."

He pulled the car to a stop in one of the parking spaces next to a menu board. "What looks good?" he asked, scanning the colorful list of choices.

"How about a strawberry slush for me," Becka said.

Ryan pushed the Call button.

"May I take your order?" a cheery voice asked.

"One medium strawberry slush and a number-two combo, please." Ryan pulled out his wallet. He looked at Becka and said, "It's my treat."

"We'll have that right out," the voice said. "Your total is $4.57."

"Thanks," Ryan said. He turned to Becka. "So what were you saying?"

Becka's heart did a somersault. She wasn't planning to talk about her feelings, at least not yet. She fidgeted with an earring as she struggled to find the right words. "I was just thinking, um, about . . . the future."

Ryan stretched. "I know what you mean."

"Really?" Her eyes widened. She wondered if he was feeling the same thing she was feeling.

"Yeah, kind of," he said. "I mean, wouldn't it be cool to know what will happen before it happens? Like, where we'll go to college, who we'll meet, what we'll do with our life and stuff like that."

"Oh." Becka was thinking more specifically about *their* future. "But don't you ever think about—"

"Hold on," Ryan said, reaching for his Bible in the backseat. He flipped through the well-worn pages. "I know what you're about to say. It says in Matthew somewhere . . . here it is in Matthew 6." He held the Bible between them.

Becka leaned forward.

Ryan pointed to verse 27. "Right here Jesus asks, 'Can all your worries add a single moment to your life? Of course not.' " Ryan paused as his eyes skimmed further down the text before he continued with verse 31. " 'So don't worry about having enough food or drink or clothing.' "

Becka cleared her throat. "Actually, what I'm trying to say is that sometimes I worry about—"

"Hold on a sec, there's more," he said. " 'Why be like the pagans who are so deeply concerned about these things? Your heavenly Father already knows all your needs, and he will give you all you need from day to day if you live for him and make the Kingdom of God your primary concern.' "

Becka blew a short breath. *Sometimes guys are just so dense,* she thought. "Ryan, that's great. And I believe it. But what I'm trying to say is . . . is that sometimes . . . well, honestly, I worry—"

"Did you hear what I just read?"

"Okay, so it was a poor choice of words," she said. Her heart danced wildly in her chest. She just had to get her feelings out in the open. "Sometimes I'm . . . *concerned* about, you know . . . *us.* About our future . . . together . . . do you know what I mean?"

Ryan's eyes met hers. Neither spoke for a long moment. Becka was sure he could hear her heart banging away. A big, melt-your-heart grin appeared on his face.

"What?" Becka said, her forehead creasing. "What are you smiling about?"

Before Ryan could answer, a teen on skates wearing a Sonic apron rolled to the edge of their car with a tray of food. "Hey, guys, sorry to interrupt. Here's your order."

~

Philip was stunned. Even now, sitting in his car outside of a local gas station, a cold chill ran down his spine as he rehearsed the events of the afternoon. He was exhausted from a fitful night's sleep. His mind was distracted by pressure from his dad. Even Krissi kind of bugged him with her questions about their future together. And yet, against the odds, he had led his school to win the regional debate championship. In fact, he had clobbered schools with much better debate teams; teams who seemed to always win. Not today.

Today, Philip blew away the competition.

What's more, the victory had come "in the near future" just as Madame Theo had predicted. But how did she know that his "star was on the rise"?

Was it a coincidence? A fluke?

Somehow he couldn't shake the feeling that there was a definite connection. Sure, at first he was skeptical about Madame Theo. But now, an hour after winning the trophy, he wasn't so quick to dismiss the messages in the tarot cards.

That's what excited and scared him the most.

Especially with that death card hanging over his head. He looked over his shoulder and spotted Scott heading toward the car. They had stopped at the minimart for a bag of chips and a couple of sodas.

"Scott, what took you so long?" Philip reached for the keys in the ignition.

Scott jumped into the front seat of Philip's convertible. "Just this," he said. He handed

Philip a strip of paper about the size of a fortune cookie fortune.

Philip started the car and then read the message.

"If that isn't the dumbest thing I've ever seen," Scott said, snatching the paper back.

Philip grunted. "What makes you say that?"

"Didn't you read it? It says, 'You will rise to the challenge today.' "

Philip appeared puzzled. "Yeah, so?" He drove away from the gas station.

"Duh," Scott said, making a face. "Rise to what challenge? Don't you see? These stupid messages are so general they could mean a million things to a million people. I can't believe people fall for this stuff."

Philip was silent for a moment. "Where did you get it?"

"Actually, I was checking my weight," Scott said, glancing out his window. "Didn't you see that scale by the door? When I stepped on it, it gave me . . . *my secret message for the day,*" Scott said in a deep, affected voice. "What a joke. As if a dumb machine is going to predict the future."

Philip clenched his jaw. He didn't like Scott's attitude. Who was to say for sure that the cosmic forces—or whatever Madame Theo had called them—couldn't communicate through that scale? If they could make contact through the cards, why not the scale, too?

"So," Scott said, guzzling his Dr. Pepper, "where did you say we're going?"

Philip hesitated, unsure what Scott would say. He was starting to regret offering Scott a ride home. No way would Scott be cool about their next stop. Then again, what choice did Philip have? He just had to know more about the second card. He tried to sound as casual as possible.

"Um, it's just a place called . . . Madame Theo's Palace."

5

ere's what I'm thinking," Fred Stoner said. He folded his arms together and, in the candlelit semi-darkness, leaned against the wall next to Madame Theo's desk. "If we're gonna boost the ratings in our new time slot, we need a fresh angle."

Madame Theo, sitting at her desk, appeared puzzled. Without warning, she felt the presence of the spirit world swirling around her. Her eyes narrowed as she attempted to process this new sensation. Who—or what—was trying to reach her? she wondered.

"Angle?" she asked, trying to remain focused.

"Yeah, you know, something to spice things up," he said.

Feeling a draft, Madame Theo glanced around the room to see if someone had entered. Again, she felt the vaporlike spirit energy drift through the air around her head. She wondered if Fred felt it, too. By the look of intensity on his face, she was pretty sure he was oblivious to the unfolding mysterious phenomenon. She tried to concentrate.

"And what do you have in mind? A guest?"

He shrugged. "Can't say for sure. Maybe." He paused to think about that for a second. "Actually, nix the guest idea. Too risky. If they're boring, we'll lose the audience."

"I see," she said, distracted by the compelling force that seemed to tug at her inner spirit. In a way she wasn't surprised that the spirit world would bypass the cards and attempt to make direct contact with her. Still, this was unlike anything she had experienced so far, and it both thrilled and, to a lesser degree, frightened her.

A moment later he snapped his fingers. "I got it. We get one of your clients to give a testimonial on camera. Yeah, that's it. We put someone on whose life has been changed or whatever from a reading. We can pretape the whole thing. I love it."

Madame Theo studied him without saying a word. The other world was there in the room. No question. The cosmic forces were trying to break through and speak directly to her consciousness. But how? What did she need to do? She closed her eyes for a long second, took a deep breath, and thought, *I'm listening. Speak.*

You have been chosen!

Madame Theo's eyes shot open. Her heart raced. The spirit guide had spoken to her. To her! Now what?

"I'm telling you, this is brilliant. There's nothing like putting a face on the benefits of the tarot," Fred said, obviously pleased with the idea.

Her head rotated slowly, from side to side, like an oscillating fan. She waited for something more, but nothing came. The presence in the room started to fade. "Wait!" she shouted as the spirit faded.

Fred almost jumped. "Excuse me?"

Madame Theo realized she had spoken out loud. "Um, sorry, it's just that . . . I'm not so sure, Fred. My clients value their privacy."

He laughed. "Have you watched TV lately? People will do just about anything for a few minutes of fame. They'll eat worms. They'll travel halfway around the world to live on an island where cameras videotape their every move. They'll even marry a complete stranger."

"Fred," Madame Theo said, her voice now quiet. Whatever had contacted her was gone, of that she was fairly sure. "I appreciate your enthusiasm. But this isn't a game show. This is very serious business."

He held up a finger. "Say no more. I agree. We'll take the high road. Don't worry. I'm not looking for cheap thrills. Just something to . . . to maximize the power of your gift."

She tapped a finger against the surface of her desk. Now, more than ever, she knew this was a gift. The spirit even said she had been chosen. "Okay, let's say I can find someone willing to go on camera. Then what? What happens if we get too much business? Have you thought of that?"

"Not to worry."

"I'm serious," she said. "I'll have you know, my schedule is already almost full with the clients I have right now."

He flashed a grin. "I know. I've got this all worked out."

She raised both eyebrows.

He rested a hand on her shoulder.

"Sweetie, this is way bigger than you can imagine. Once we syndicate, thousands— maybe millions—of people will want what you have to offer."

"And, pray tell, how do you propose I handle that?"

"You don't." Fred rubbed his hands together. "As of tonight, we start pushing a toll-free number for personal consultations. I've made arrangements with a phone bank in Salt Lake City who will field the calls."

Madame Theo squinted. "I . . . I don't know. Readings by phone?" Would the collective spirit world be offended by such a thing? she wondered.

"Exactly." Fred started to pace. "The first minute of the consultation is $5.95 and then $1 a minute after that. If the average call is ten minutes, we're talking almost $15 per call. Do the math. A thousand ten-minute calls is $15,000. At that rate, we're talking $90,000 per hour."

She whistled, warming to the idea. Surely there was nothing wrong with introducing people to the supernatural, right? If she made a lot of money along the way, the spirits would have to guide her on how to use it for the greater good.

"That's just the start," he said. "People who want a personal reading from you will have to pay more."

"What's the catch?"

"No catch." Fred suppressed a cough. "But, as you might guess, I do need the green light to syndicate into Los Angeles for the deal to work."

Madame Theo fell silent. In the other room, the bell above the front door jingled, indicating someone was entering. Besides, she needed time to process what had just happened. Never before had she been spoken to by the other side so directly.

"Fred, I have a client. I . . . I better go."

He circled around and faced her. "What's the problem? I thought you'd be thrilled."

"I am, it's just—"

"Los Angeles," he said, finishing her sentence. "I don't get it. What is your objection to doing TV in LA?"

She pushed herself back from the desk and then stood. "I wish I could tell you, Fred. But I can't. Maybe later."

"Like, when? I've got a show to run."

"Soon."

∿

Scott tagged behind Philip as they headed into Madame Theo's Palace. Once inside, a heaviness of heart, like a dark cloud, settled over Scott. He couldn't shake the distinct impression that they shouldn't be there. He wasn't able to pinpoint the source of his uneasiness. He didn't know the first thing about Madame Theo, her store, or tarot cards. But the restlessness in his spirit was as distinct as the cinnamon incense that filled the air.

"This place gives me the creeps," Scott said just above a whisper.

Philip, standing inside the door, turned around and shot him a look. "Like I said, you can wait outside if you're going to make a bunch of comments."

"Hey, it's your show," Scott said, scanning the room. As his vision adjusted to the meager light, he noticed the table situated in the center of the room, the candles, the thick bloodred-colored drapes, and the incense pot. What really caught his eye was the array of crystals displayed on the end table in the far corner. *Not good,* he thought.

Scott and his sister, Becka, had been engaged in enough spiritual warfare to know the warning signs early on. Anybody who turned to crystals for guidance was asking for trouble, and he knew it. Scott looked at Philip and was about to caution him when a woman appeared through the beaded doorway.

"Welcome," she said, offering a polite smile.

"Uh, hi," Philip said, inching forward. "Remember me? From yesterday?"

She nodded. "I do. Please have a seat, Philip. And who is this with you?"

Scott cleared his throat. He remained standing close to the door, unwilling to venture too close. The alarms in his head seemed to grow with each passing minute. "I'm Scott. Scott Williams."

Madame Theo drifted like a phantom to her chair. She floated into place and rested her hands on the table. "I take it, Scott, you're not here for a reading?"

He shook his head. "No, ma'am. I'm here with my friend."

She closed her eyes. When she opened them several seconds later, she appeared agitated. "I'm sorry, Scott. I need to ask you to wait outside."

"Me?" he said, raising a hand to his chest. "What did I do?"

"Please," she said firmly. "We won't be long."

"I don't get it," Scott said, his face flushed. "Why can't I stay right here?"

Philip's head spun around. "Don't make a scene, Scott. Just do what she says."

Scott felt his pulse race. It wasn't that he wanted to stay, but he didn't like being asked to leave for no apparent reason. Besides, what right did she have to judge him? Scott fumed, "Let me guess, I've got *bad karma*? Is that it?"

Madame Theo tilted her head to the side. "In a word, yes. Your karma is competing with the cosmic realities necessary to offer a proper reading of the cards."

"Whatever," Scott said, shaking his head. With a turn, he opened the door and stepped outside. He yanked the door shut with a sharp thwack. Almost instantly, he regretted leaving Philip alone with that woman. Philip wasn't a believer, and Scott knew full well that he would be putty in the hands of the great deceiver. Now what? Should he go back inside? What would he say?

∾

Scott sat in the front seat of the car, troubled by what had just happened. He knew he probably ticked Philip off inside of Madame Theo's. He didn't mean to, but he couldn't help himself. For the life of him, he couldn't think of a single reason why Madame Theo asked him to leave.

In fact, for the last fifteen minutes, he replayed the brief sequence of events. The only thing he remembered saying was his name—and that Philip was a friend. That's it. After Madame Theo had closed her eyes, she told him to leave.

Talk about weird, Scott thought. But on second thought, Scott felt convicted for acting so selfishly. He had been obsessed with staying on Philip's good side. Instead, Scott realized he should be more concerned that Philip felt the need to go to such a creepy place.

At the moment, he watched Philip storm toward the car and braced himself for the worst.

"You wanna know something?" Philip shouted as he reached the side of the vehicle. He jumped in and then slammed the car door shut with enough force to rattle the rearview mirror.

"What's that?"

"*Sometimes* you can be such a *complete* jerk." That said, Philip jammed in the key and stomped on the gas pedal.

"That's good," Scott said with a smirk. "For a second I thought you were going to announce that I was *always* a jerk."

"Back off, Scott," Philip said. He gripped the steering wheel and looked straight ahead.

Scott let out a low whistle. "Hey, I'm just playing with you. Now who's got the bad karma?"

Rather than say another word, Philip cranked the volume on the radio until it was almost deafening.

"Hey, you want to turn that down?" Scott shouted.

"No."

"Come on, man. Let's talk."

Philip turned the music up a notch.

Scott reached over and snapped it off.

Philip's eyes narrowed into a glare, but he didn't say a word.

"Listen, Philip, I'm sorry that—"

He cut Scott off. "I don't want to talk about it."

"Okay . . . okay. Chill out, man."

They rode several minutes in the silence. Scott had never seen Philip so on edge. Yesterday in the lunch room had come close. But this was different. Philip's whole temperament was changing. He had a wild, faraway look in his eyes.

A new thought came to mind. Maybe Philip had heard something inside that frightened him. Maybe. But what? What could possibly be so disturbing that it would cause Philip to be so on edge? If only he knew more about tarot cards, then perhaps he'd know what Philip was getting mixed up in.

One thing was sure. Scott would ask Z when he got home. Although Scott didn't know much about Z, it seemed that Z had tons of advice about these kinds of things, especially if it had to do with the spirit realm.

"You know," Scott said, trying to start a conversation, "I actually think it would be kind of cool to know the future . . . and all of that stuff."

Philip clenched his jaw and stared straight ahead.

"I'm serious," Scott added, trying to sound sincere. "You know, that would make it easier to figure out what to do before you had to do it, right?"

Philip looked the other way.

"But if you ask me—," Scott started to say.

Philip's head snapped around. His eyes were as dark as his hair. "I didn't *ask* you."

"Still," Scott said, ignoring him, "there's something not right with that lady. Her whole deal is so . . . weird, you know? I mean, the candles, the crystals, the turban thing around her head—what's with that, anyway?"

Philip slammed on his brakes. The car skidded to a stop. "Get out."

"What?"

"Now."

"Here? Why?"

Philip barked, "You just don't know when to shut up, do you?"

6

*B*ecka hummed
a tuneless melody as she, gliding through the
kitchen, stacked the spaghetti-soiled dinner
plates in the sink. Nothing could dampen
the feeling of euphoria. Not the pile of
homework awaiting her in her bedroom, not
the fact that she had to study for two tests,
not even Scott's sour mood.

Today was an exceptional day. Her mom,

who needed to rush out after dinner for a meeting at church, had asked her to do the dishes. Becka didn't mind. All she cared about was what happened that afternoon at Sonic.

With Ryan.

As she rehearsed every little detail, she was amazed that her heart didn't go into cardiac arrest when Ryan had said he, too, was thinking about their future *together*. True, they had always taken their relationship slowly. Still, he had feelings for her. What more could she want? Knowing that was enough to put the spin in her world.

Her spirit soared somewhere above the clouds at the memory.

From some faraway place, she thought she heard a voice calling her name . . . *Becka*.

Gazing at the sunset, its golden glow perfectly framed through the window over the sink, she lowered a dish into the warm water. As her hands slipped into the soap bubbles, her mind drifted miles away to the ocean. She imagined herself on the beach walking along the seaside with her toes leaving little tracks in the sand.

With Ryan.

"Becka . . ."

This time, the voice was much clearer. She blinked and found herself in front of the sink. She sighed as reality set back in. Out of the corner of her eye, she spotted her mother by the front door, purse and keys in hand. "Oh, hey, Mom."

"Didn't you hear me calling your name, sweetheart?"

"I . . . I guess I was lost in my thoughts," Becka said, blushing.

"I've got the cell phone in case you guys need anything, okay?"

"We'll be fine, Mom," Becka said, noticing her hands were dripping onto the floor. She quickly placed them over the sink.

"I'll be back in about two hours," Mrs. Williams said. "Thanks for doing the dishes, Becka. And, Scott?"

He grunted, "Yeah, Mom?"

"Don't forget tonight is trash night—"

"I know, I'll handle it."

Mrs. Williams hesitated with one hand on the doorknob. "Well, better run. How do I look?"

Becka tilted her head. "Great, Mom. I really like your new dress."

That brought a smile. "Thanks, sweetie. I love you both," she said and then left.

Becka's attention drifted from the front door to the lump of humanity hunched over his plate at the kitchen table. From experience, she knew something was seriously wrong if Scott refused to eat. Especially if he was ignoring something as awesome as Mom's homemade spaghetti and meatballs.

Ever since their father had died in a plane crash while on the mission field in South America, she and Scott had drawn closer. In many ways, they were the best of friends even though he was two years younger. When he was hurting, Becka hurt with him.

She forced herself to put her daydream on hold, dried her hands on a towel, walked to the table, and pulled up a chair. "So what's up, bro?"

Scott noodled his spaghetti with a fork. He shrugged.

"Come on, Scotty," she said, pulling her hair back. "Are you bummed out that Philip won first place in the debate?"

He looked up. "No way. I'm happy for him."

"Then why the long face?" As she waited for Scott to respond, Muttly wandered into the room and rested at Becka's feet. Becka leaned over and rubbed his belly.

Scott leaned back in his chair and folded his arms. "Philip's being a dork, big time."

"Okay, like how?"

Scott shook his head in disgust. "Get this. He kicked me out of the car and made me walk almost halfway home."

Oddly, that actually struck her as funny. She bit her bottom lip to suppress a laugh. "You're kidding, right?"

"For real. The guy's nuts in the head," Scott said, making cuckoo circles next to his ear. "He slammed on the brakes, which just about killed us. Then he yelled and told me to get out of the car. He's so messed up."

Becka, still fighting back a snicker, said, "Mom and I wondered what took you so long to get home."

"Actually, we stopped at some Madame Weirdo's place first."

"Huh?" Becka watched as Muttly stretched his legs and then strolled out of the room, apparently losing interest in the conversation.

"She's a lady that tells the future with tarot cards—whatever they are," Scott said. He reached for a roll. "At least that's what Philip claims." He munched on the bread for a second.

Becka didn't like the sound of Philip getting mixed up with a fortune-teller. Although she was no expert on the subject, she knew enough about the Bible and had come face-to-face with demonic powers to know that stuff like palm reading and fooling around with contacting spirits was a bad deal. "Do you think that this what's-her-face—"

"Madame Theo," Scott said, as a picture of her turban-bound head came to mind.

"Yeah, that this Madame Theo might have something to do with Philip's reaction?"

"I don't know. Probably." Scott popped the

rest of the roll into his mouth. "At least, it looks that way, now that you mention it."

Becka sat cross-legged on the chair. "I know. Why don't you just call and talk to Krissi? Maybe she knows what's up with Philip."

"You think so?"

"Sure. I mean, this involves Krissi, too."

"How's that?"

"Think about it," Becka said. "Philip was so not himself yesterday in the cafeteria, right?"

"Yeah. So?"

"I say there's a connection between what happened today and what was going on yesterday. See?"

"I . . ."

"Trust me," Becka said, starting to stand. "Just call it a woman's intuition."

"But what do I tell Krissi?" Scott said, scrunching his nose. "I don't know the first thing about tarot cards."

"Why not ask Z first?"

Scott smacked his forehead. "I knew there was something I forgot to do. I'll see if he's on-line."

Scott walked into his bedroom and quietly turned on the small desk lamp. Cornelius, his pet military macaw, stood asleep on a perch near his desk. With one foot drawn to his chest, his powerful beak was buried in a patch of bright green and scarlet plumage. Scott scratched the back of his bird's neck before taking a seat in front of the computer.

Scott tapped the space bar to wake the monitor from its sleep mode. He typed in his password—Dirty Socks—and logged on to the computer. After many months, they were no closer to knowing much about the mysterious Z, even though on several occasions they had tried to discover Z's true identity.

One thing was certain: Z was an expert on the supernatural and for some strange reason had taken an interest in Scott and Becka's efforts to fight the forces of darkness. Whenever they had a question about the occult, they'd send Z an e-mail. Often Z would be on-line in the evenings. Scott noted the clock on his menu bar: 8:47. His fingers danced across the keyboard.

Hey, Z. Are you there? It's Scott.

As Scott waited, he couldn't help but think of all of the things Z knew about them . . . personal family things. In a way, it was unsettling. Z knew stuff that only somebody really close to them could know. So far, Z had never steered them wrong or done anything to make them uncomfortable.

Still, the fact that this stranger knew about him and seemed to care about him was diffi-

cult for Scott to process. In an odd sort of
way, Z made Scott long for his dad. His dad,
after all, was someone who, like Z, knew a lot
about the Bible and who always helped him
figure stuff out.

Scott watched a response form on the
screen.

> *Great to hear from you,*
> *Scott. How's your friend?*

Scott swallowed. He assumed Z was refer-
ring to Philip. *How in the world does Z know
about him?* Scott thought. He hadn't said anything about Philip, at least not yet. That eerie
sensation returned, but Scott shrugged it off.
Z just seemed to have his sources. Scott typed:

> Z, Philip is really stressed out. He's using tarot
> cards to figure out the future. What do you
> know about tarot?

After several seconds, a message from Z
appeared:

> *Tarot cards are nothing more than a tool*
> *of divination used to foretell events, much like*
> *crystal gazing, palmistry, or soothsaying.*

> Is it dangerous?

> *Indeed. On several levels.*

Like how?

Scott waited as his cursor blinked impatiently on the screen. No response.

Z, I have to know. What's Philip getting into?

After a pause, an answer appeared:

People who promote tarot cards claim it's an innocent way to discern the future. They use words like spiritual development, inner knowledge, life forces, *and* cosmic energies *to explain what you're tapping into with the cards.*

So what's the danger?

Another extended pause. Scott took a deep breath. He knew sometimes Z wouldn't answer a direct question, at least not immediately. And other times, Z would answer a question with a question. A question formed on the screen:

Who holds your life in his hand?

That's easy. Jesus does.

Who knows everything about your future?

Jesus.

How does he invite you to communicate with him?

By talking with him. Through prayer. What's this
got to do with tarot cards?

As Scott waited for a response, Becka
walked into the room and leaned over his
shoulder. "What's Z saying?"

"I'm a little confused," Scott said, scratch-
ing the side of his head. "I don't think he
really answered my question."

"Let's see," Becka said, reaching for the
mouse. She scrolled back and read the conversation thread. "Hey, I think I get what Z's
trying to say."

"Okay, if you're so brilliant, what's he saying?"

"You've got to read between the lines,
Scott. Look here." She pointed to the screen.
"We're supposed to talk to Jesus through
prayer, right?"

"Right . . . but . . ."

"Which means we don't need tarot cards,"
Becka said. "We already have a direct line to
God. So who, then, are people talking to
when they use stuff like tarot cards to com-
municate? It sure can't be God. Get it? That's
Z's point."

"I guess . . . but . . ."

Becka nudged Scott to the side and typed
a question:

Z, it's Becka. Are you saying that tarot cards can open up a person to satanic activity?

They waited several seconds before one word appeared on the screen:

Exactly.

Scott felt a sudden chill creep up from the base of his spine. If tarot cards were really just another form of spiritual counterfeit, one with roots in the occult, then Philip was in more danger than he probably knew. Even though Scott was still hacked off at Philip for kicking him out of the car, there was no way he'd stand by and let his friend get sucked into a trap.

Scott pounded out one last question:

Z, it's Scott. I've got to know. How dangerous are they?

Nothing. Scott exchanged a look with Becka. He checked the screen again. After what felt like forever, Z's response scrawled across the screen one letter at a time:

Can be lethal.

Z

7

_S_peaking of lover boy," Scott said, lowering his voice to Krissi the next day before study hall. He nodded in the direction of the door.

Krissi, who sat next to Scott, looked over his shoulder as Philip shuffled into the crowded study hall. His T-shirt was partially untucked in the back, his jeans wrinkled, and his hair had a bad case of static cling.

He took one of the remaining available seats in the front right corner of the room close to the door. Not that he had much of a choice. All of the seats in the back were already taken. Philip flopped into his chair, plopped his stuff on the desk in front of him, and leaning forward, dropped his chin onto the stack of books.

"I'd say he had five minutes of sleep last night," Scott said, leaning closer to Krissi. "Five minutes, tops. I told you something's up with him. I bet he was up in the middle of the night watching that Madame Whacko I was telling you about."

Krissi's eyelashes fluttered. "Really? Okay, you've got to tell me all about this place you guys, like, went to after school. And don't skip anything."

Last night, at Becka's suggestion, Scott had planned to call Krissi to talk about Philip. As usual, Scott got distracted and forgot. After first period, he caught up with her and made a plan to talk with her during this study hall.

The bell sounded and, as Scott started to answer, the librarian stepped into the room. "What's Mr. Lowry doing here?"

Krissi tossed her auburn hair. "Beats me. I almost never see him doing study hall duty, you know?"

Scott nodded. "Well, he's cool. The last

time I was in detention, he let us talk as long as we didn't cause a riot."

Mr. Lowry stood at the front of the room tapping a thin, black attendance book against his thigh. Scott noticed most of the other students ignored his presence. This was, after all, a talking study hall. Unlike the silent study hall in room 305, where conversation was forbidden, Scott knew the students here were normally allowed to talk as long as they kept the general noise level lower than a sonic boom.

"May I have your attention," Mr. Lowry announced, mustering up a commanding voice.

A girl with thick glasses turned in her seat and started to shush the others.

"As you may have guessed, I'm a substitute teacher for this period." He circled around the teacher's desk and leaned against the front edge. "I understand that this is usually a talking period. Today, however, will be different."

Several students groaned.

Mr. Lowry started to pace back and forth at the front of the class as if addressing the troops. "As of this moment, there will be no talking—"

More groans.

"No talking . . . no eating . . . no sleeping—"

Another round of whines and moans.

"And there will be no passing of notes," he said, pointing with the black attendance book like a battle-ax.

One of the jocks on the basketball team blurted, "Mr. Lowry?"

"Yes?"

The jock leaned back in his chair, legs sprawled as if in a lounge chair at the beach. "Um, sir. In case they didn't tell you, this isn't junior high."

Several of his buddies snickered.

"What's next? No gum chewing?" he added with a laugh.

Mr. Lowry stared at him as if torn between ordering him to do five hundred push-ups or settling for a swift boot to the seat of his pants. "Young man, what is your name?"

He looked around as if Mr. Lowry were addressing someone else and then said, "Who, me?"

He marched forward three steps. "I'm waiting."

Every eye in the room was on him. The student cleared his throat. "Jordan Bolte."

"Thank you, Mr. Bolte, for that wonderful idea." Mr. Lowry turned to face the others. "At the suggestion of Mr. Bolte, there will be no gum chewing, either."

"Oh, that's great, Jordy," one of his buddies said, with a punch to his arm.

"For those students with pagers, cell

phones, or instant messengers," he said, scanning the faces through narrowed eyes, "if you want to keep them, I'd suggest you turn them off and put them away. Thank you. I have a pounding migraine headache and will not tolerate any extraneous noise." Mr. Lowry took a seat behind the desk and opened the roll book. He started to take attendance.

Scott exchanged a look with Krissi. Scott whispered, "What came over him?"

Krissi shrugged and then silently mouthed the words, *Now what?*

Scott threw up his hands. He hadn't planned on this curveball. Whatever Mr. Lowry's reason, which, for obvious reasons, Scott wouldn't dare question, the option of talking was nixed.

Krissi took out a sheet of paper and a pen. She motioned to him to do the same.

Scott wasn't sure that was such a good idea. Without speaking, he mouthed back, "Pass a note?" What if they got caught? If only he had remembered to call her last night.

He looked into Krissi's pleading, green eyes and guessed that if he didn't tell her what he knew, Krissi would nag him through the entire forty-five-minute period. What harm could there be in telling her the basics? Besides, Mr. Lowry, he reasoned, was a substitute study-hall teacher—a tough one, sure.

But he was a seasoned student. He knew all the tricks of silent communication.

What were the odds of being noticed in the last row?

He slipped out a piece of paper, clicked open his pen, and began to write in large block type, stealing quick glances in the direction of the teacher. As he worked, his heart started to pound. The last thing he needed was another detention. When he finished, he propped up a textbook and, with a suppressed cough, signaled to Krissi.

Krissi, trying not to be too obvious, tilted her head. She squinted. Scott lifted the paper for a better view behind the book. She squinted again but couldn't read it. Frustrated, Scott pretended to look at the ceiling and then the bulletin board before scanning the front of the room.

Mr. Lowry's head was down as he called names and scrawled marks in the attendance book.

Krissi tapped her pen twice. Scott looked at her as her eyes widened, as if to ask, "Are you going to give that to me or not?"

Scott's heart tapped away. He knew he was taking a risk. A big risk. No way would he want anybody but Krissi to see what he had written. Against his better judgment, he carefully folded the paper several times. His movements were slow and deliberate so as to attract as little attention as possible. When finished, the paper fit in the palm of his hand.

He stole a final look at the teacher and then sniffled.

As if on cue, Krissi pretended to accidentally knock her pen onto the floor between them. It rolled toward Scott. As smooth as a well-rehearsed play, Scott picked up the pen and handed it to Krissi, slipping the note into her hand in the same motion.

Although the adrenaline was pumping through his veins, Scott lowered his book, satisfied that they had pulled it off. He exhaled a slow, long breath.

Several seconds passed when, from across the room, he thought he heard someone say, "I'll take that."

Scott's heart skipped a beat. No mistake about it. Mr. Lowry's eyes, like two laser-guided missiles, zeroed in on Krissi.

"Excuse me?" Krissi said, playing dumb. She tried to smile.

With a wave of the hand, Mr. Lowry beckoned. "I may spend most of my time in a library, but I wasn't born yesterday. Hand me the note."

"I . . . I just—"

"Now, please."

Krissi looked at Scott and winced. Her otherwise fair complexion reddened. As she walked to the front of the class, he knew they were busted. Big time. Talk about a bad dream. Make that a nightmare. Krissi dropped the note on the desk and turned to leave.

"Don't move. Remain by my desk," Mr. Lowry said, promptly unfolding the page.

The clock on the wall ticked away a painfully long minute. *If only the floor would open up and swallow me,* Scott thought, burying his face in his hands.

With a jerk, Mr. Lowry stood up and faced the class. "I'd like for the person who wrote this to join her."

Scott tried to swallow, but his throat was as dry as sand.

At first, he didn't move—couldn't move was more like it. His feet felt as if they were encased in cement. What choice did he have? Every eye in the room was on him. He inched out of his seat and sulked his way to the front. The room was so quiet, Scott could hear the blood throbbing along the edge of his earlobes.

"People," Mr. Lowry said, obviously delighted to enforce the rules, "this is how we handle those who can't follow basic instructions."

Scott took his place alongside Krissi, drooping his shoulders as if waiting to be court-martialed. From the corner of his eye, he couldn't help but see the angry scowl on Philip's face. Scott looked away. He tried to focus on a spot on the floor instead. His mind ran wild. *Whatever you do . . . starve me . . . use Chinese torture on me . . . just don't read that out loud.*

Mr. Lowry raised the note for all to see, as if holding the scalp of someone from a warring tribe. He lowered the paper and held it at arm's length. "I now have something to share with the group."

Scott stopped breathing. *Oh, great, I'm so dead,* he thought. *Looks like for once Krissi won't be blamed for starting the rumors.*

Mr. Lowry adjusted his reading glasses. He began to read the note out loud. " 'Krissi, you know how much Philip is changing? Well, I think he's depressed. Like, big time. He tries to look like he has it together, but I think he's losing it. He even went to a psychic yesterday. That's messed up. As if a lady in a turban really knows anything about the future. That just shows you how desperate he must be. I think he needs you now more than ever . . .' " Mr. Lowry stopped. "I think that's about enough," he said, crumpling the note in his hand.

Yeah, Scott thought, *enough for Philip to want to skin me alive.*

8

The white FedEx truck stopped in the middle of the road, its flashers on. The driver, wearing shorts, clutching a clipboard and an eight-by-ten flat envelope, hopped out. She hustled to the building and rang the bell.

The door opened. "Yes?"

"Hi. Package for—" The driver paused to

scan the label, then added, "For a Rita Thomas."

At the sound of Rita's name, a brief spike of fear surged in Madame Theo's heart. Instinctively, she peeked up and down the street to see if anyone might overhear the conversation. She knew she couldn't be too careful.

"Yes . . . thank you, that's me," Madame Theo said, reaching for the clipboard. She kept inside the door, her heart still jumpy.

"I'll need your signature right there," the driver said, pointing toward the bottom half of the form. "And, if you would, print your name next to it . . . on the second line."

Madame Theo carefully filled in the required information with the pen attached to the clipboard.

"Nice day, isn't it?" the driver said, making small talk while Madame Theo took her time signing the document as if she were creating a work of art. "I hear they're calling for rain."

"We could use some, couldn't we?" Madame Theo said, putting the finishing touches on her masterpiece. She looked up. "Here you go."

"Thank you very much," the driver said, retrieving the clipboard. Using a handheld scanner, she swiped the bar code on the label, typed in the date and time on the side of the scanning device, and then holstered it like a gun on her belt. She started to hand over the envelope when, for no apparent reason, she stopped and took a good look at Madame Theo.

Madame Theo, her hand extended to receive the package, returned the gaze. She raised an eyebrow wondering what was wrong. Why didn't the FedEx lady give her the envelope?

"You want to know something funny?"

Madame Theo pretended to be interested. "What's that?"

"It's just that your face looks really familiar." The woman tucked the clipboard under an arm. She made no further effort to release the envelope. "Aren't you on TV?"

Madame Theo felt her face flush. *Where is this going?* "Yes, such as it is," she answered, her posture matter-of-fact. "We're on in the middle of the night, for now, that is."

"That's it," the driver said with a broad smile. "The other night I couldn't sleep. My husband was out of town, and I always have a hard time falling asleep when he's away. Anyway, that's when I must have seen you on TV."

Although not an impatient person, Madame Theo was growing restless. She was dying to review the material from her former lawyer. She kept an eye on the package, like a vulture eyeing its next meal, and forced a smile. "I'm glad to know there's at least one person in the audience watching. Now, if you don't mind, I had better get back to work."

Perplexed, the driver tilted her head to one side.

"Is there something wrong?" Madame Theo asked.

"Actually, before I can leave this with you," the driver said, withholding the envelope, "I'll need to see some form of picture ID from you, ma'am."

"Excuse me?" Madame Theo's heart skipped several beats. "I . . . is that necessary?"

"You see this little orange sticker?" she said, holding up the package as if presenting evidence to the jury. "I can only leave this with the person who's named therein."

"So?"

"You signed this as Rita Thomas."

"Indeed. That's me."

"But last night, on TV, you were Madame Theo."

Madame Theo tucked a loose strand of hair back underneath her turban. She was beginning to see where this was going and started to steam. Why did her lawyer put Rita's name on it? He, of all people, should know a move like that would cause complications. Now what?

"You see," the psychic said in a soft, confidential voice, "Madame Theo is my . . . my stage name. So I'll just take that and we'll move on, okay? I'm expecting a client any moment."

"I still need to see some form of ID," the woman said, her tone pleasant but firm. "Driver's license. Passport. Just something with a picture. It's company policy."

Madame Theo sighed.

"I'm sure you know we do this for your security. Must be important stuff if it's got one of those orange stickers."

What was the point of arguing? Madame Theo ducked back inside the room, fished her wallet out of her frumpy, oversize bag, and returned to the door. With a flip, she opened the flap and presented her California driver's license.

"Nice picture," the FedEx lady said, studying the two-by-three plastic card. "Says here you're Theodella Smith."

A nod. "Naturally, in my line of work, I go by Madame Theo. But, yes, that's my full name."

The FedEx service woman handed back the license.

"What about the package?" Madame Theo asked, expectant, trying not to sound too anxious.

"I'm really sorry, ma'am. Unless you have another picture ID bearing the name of Rita

Thomas, I'll need to return this to the station."

Madame Theo shook her head in disbelief. She was jammed between the desperate need to get that package and the reality that she, decades ago, had erased all traces of her former self, the lovely Rita Thomas. She didn't have a single item with Rita's name on it. Certainly not a picture ID. What if somebody broke in, snooped through her stuff, and stumbled on it? She'd be through. Or what if she were raided by the police?

Like the last time?

Still, Madame Theo had to find a way to put her hands on that information. With it, maybe she'd be able to convince her producer, Fred Stoner, to end his relentless push to syndicate into Los Angeles.

She tried another approach. "I . . . well, can't you make an exception? After all, I am on TV. You can trust me."

"You could be one of the Beatles," the driver said with a guarded smile. "Still, as long as there's an orange sticker, we have no choice but to verify your ID."

Madame Theo started to feel dizzy. "Are you sure?"

"I'll tell you what," the driver said, extending a business card. "That's the dispatcher's number. Call him. I doubt it, but maybe you can work something out. Sorry. Gotta run."

With that, she turned and dashed to the truck.

Within seconds, Madame Theo was at her desk. She dialed a private number and waited for an answer.

On the fourth ring, her lawyer muttered, "Zack Zimmerman."

Madame Theo clutched the phone against the side of her head. "What kind of stunt are you pulling, Zack?"

The bell sounded, signaling the end of fourth period. Contrary to what he had envisioned, Scott discovered he was still alive. The floor hadn't swallowed him. The walls hadn't crushed him. And he hadn't been publicly stoned for what he had done—at least not yet. Somehow he managed to survive the snickers, the catcalls, and the sneers from the students while Mr. Lowry read his note.

Philip was another matter. The instant the bell rang, he ducked out the door and, like a phantom, disappeared into the crowded hallway. Scott, with Krissi in tow, pushed their way through the mass of bodies and headed for the cafeteria. Getting there was like trying to make their way through rush-hour traffic.

Krissi tapped Scott's arm. "You think he's mad?"

"You're kidding, right?"

"Well, it wasn't like we were trying to be mean—"

"Doesn't matter," Scott said. "Didn't you see the look on his face while Mr. Lowry started reading?"

Krissi sighed. "Yeah, I feel really bad for him."

A moment later, they reached the food line, grabbed trays, silverware, napkins and then slinked forward to select their lunch choices. Philip, coming from the opposite direction, walked toward them. With a shove to Scott's shoulder, he said, "Boy, you sure can't be trusted, can you?"

Scott knew he deserved the rebuke and didn't shove back. As a kid, whenever Scott would get into a scuffle, his dad would say, "Remember, son, blessed are the peacemakers." Now was one of those times he needed to practice a healthy dose of grace.

"Did you ever think," Philip said, his eyes puffy, "about asking for my permission before talking behind my back?"

Scott held his tongue. For one of the first times in his life, Scott had nothing to say.

"Well, did you?"

Krissi, however, spoke up. "Come on, Philip. I asked Scott about yesterday because I'm concerned about you. How did we know the teacher would do that?"

"Krissi," Philip said with a sigh, "I really do think this is between Scott and me. You and I can talk about things later, okay?"

Scott started to apologize. "Man, I . . . I'm—"

Philip cut him off. "A creep, that's what you are, Scott Williams." Philip inched closer. "In fact, you're the biggest chump in the world." With that, Philip turned and started to leave. Three steps away he paused, then turned back around. "What kind of Christian are you, anyway?"

9

The sun struggled to poke a hole through the gray clouds that hung, like a thick blanket, low in the sky. It would be raining before long, of that Philip was sure. He pulled his convertible to a stop and parked directly in front of Madame Theo's Palace. Thanks to Scott and Krissi's blunder, he no longer felt the need to hide what he was doing from friends at school.

By the time lunch was over, the buzz in the hallway was about Philip and the TV psychic. The rumor mill was working overtime. Everywhere he walked, he heard whispers and felt as if people everywhere were now talking behind his back. And once, while using the bathroom, he had overheard some punk telling his buddy a joke about Madame Theo:

"Knock knock."

"Who's there?"

"Madame Theo."

"Madame Theo who?"

"If you were psychic, you'd know, too."

It wasn't even funny, Philip thought, dismissing the memory.

He raised the top on his convertible and, checking his watch, noticed he was right on time for his hastily scheduled appointment. After today's meltdown at school, he knew he needed to get some clarity. And so far, in spite of what the others might say about her, Madame Theo was right on the money. His mind drifted back to the three-card spread she had dealt during his initial session.

According to the first tarot card, she predicted his star was on the rise. The next day he won the debate against the best team in the region. At first he had wondered if it was a mere coincidence. In light of the current developments, he wasn't so sure. Last night, he was contacted by a recruiter from one of the colleges he was really interested in. Somehow they had gotten wind of his performance and quickly arranged an increase in their scholarship offer.

The second card, the one with people leaping from the tower, indicated he should make some drastic changes. *That's easy,* he thought. After today, he could see that he needed to cut things off with Krissi and especially with Scott. Philip was convinced they'd do nothing but hold him back. Or worse. Their friendship could keep his star from rising further and might even contribute to his downfall.

But it was the third card, the death card, that worried him at the moment. If Madame Theo was right about the first two cards, then she was most likely on target with the third. Was he going to die? Was someone close to him going to die? Or, as she had hinted, was there something in his world that needed to end for him to advance in his climb to the top? He needed to know. He needed someone to talk with who wouldn't mock his desire to know the future.

He needed Madame Theo. Or did he? So far, she seemed to have all the answers. Maybe that was part of what was bothering him. Maybe he was giving her too much credit. What if everything she had predicted about his future was just a coincidence?

Then again, what harm was there in giving her another chance? Philip reached for the handle and let himself in.

"Please, Philip, come in. I've been expecting you," she said, already sitting at the table.

It took a moment for him to adjust to the blast of scented air and the darkness of the room. He took a seat across from Madame Theo and, with a sigh, slumped forward.

"I see a young man with a heavy heart," she said. Her voice was soft and airy as a feather.

Philip took a deep breath. "I . . . I hope I'm not late."

She shook her head. "You're right on time, my friend. Now give me your hands." She extended her hands, palms up, across the table. "Why don't you start by telling me what's troubling your spirit."

For a split second, Philip felt a little alarm go off in the back of his brain. It warned something wasn't right, a warning that he promptly dismissed. He slipped his hands into hers and tried to think where he should start.

In the quiet that followed, he felt moved to come clean. He confessed his original doubts about her, about the cards, about the whole idea that she could actually discern future events. He told her about winning the debate, about losing his girlfriend—and the fallout with Scott. And he told her about his fears of the death card.

As he spoke, Madame Theo's eyes remained closed, her grip steady and firm. She seemed to be in a trance. Without warning, she released his hands and looked him straight in the eyes. "This evening," she announced, dropping her arms below the table, "I believe you're ready for the next level."

"Come again?"

"At first, by your own admission, you didn't believe with your whole heart. Your mind refused to give way to your deeper, inner connection to the spirit realm. I see that has changed." Madame Theo reached for the deck of tarot cards. "This change is good. This is very good, Philip."

He smiled at the affirmation.

"I knew when I first saw you, you were destined for greatness," she added, covering the deck with the palm of her hand.

Philip straightened up in his chair. He liked the sound of her validation. "Um, thank you," was all he could think to say.

"Now keep in mind," she said, "each reading relies upon the kinetic forces operating in the universe at the time of the reading."

"Got it." Philip vaguely remembered this from their first session.

"Which means your concerns about the death card will either be validated, deepened, or changed, depending on the ebb and flow of the unseen divine forces."

"Okay," Philip said, unsure if this was good news or bad.

"Before we begin, let us invoke the goodness of the eternal spirit guide," she said, closing her eyes, her hands still hovering over the cards.

"Huh? Oh," Philip said, figuring out that he, too, should probably bow his head. Once again, a little alarm sounded in his mind, although less strongly this time. He shoved it aside.

"May the highest powers be pleased by our desire for good, not harm, to come of this revelation. We stand against the negative forces that might thwart a blessing. So be it."

Philip peeked with one eye, unsure if it was okay to look. "Uh . . . amen," he said quickly, uncertain what the right response should be to her quasi prayer. He watched as Madame Theo dealt five cards in a straight row, facedown in the center of the table.

"This is a five-card spread," she said, setting the balance of the deck to one side. "The meanings are similar to the three-card spread. But there are differences."

"How so?"

"We start with the past influences," she

said, turning over the first. It revealed a man and woman standing in a garden. "Hmm. These are the lovers. In the past, you've been close to someone special. She has held much influence over you. And now you must decide if you will remain under her influence. Can you think of someone who this might represent?"

Philip immediately said, "Krissi."

"Your girlfriend, the one you're broken up with, at least in your heart?"

A nod.

"Good. It appears the cards are confirming your need for a change." She turned over the second tarot card. "This is your present influence."

"Looks like a dude in a chariot," Philip said, tilting his head for a better view.

"Strictly speaking, yes. What it represents has much to do with the tension of opposite forces at work."

"I . . . I . . . what's that mean?"

"Could be pointing to a divorce," Madame Theo said, carefully eyeing Philip's reaction.

"Wow. My parents are split up . . ."

"That, Philip, must be the opposite forces at work in your life. The cards are saying you must remain steady in the midst of the struggle."

"I see." Philip felt his heart racing. He had watched her shuffle the deck. How, then, did the cards know his situation? With each second, Philip found himself longing to understand and to connect with whatever was at work behind the cards.

When Madame Theo dealt the third card, Philip gasped. "That guy looks like he's been hanged," he said, his voice cracking midsentence. "What in the world—"

"Not to worry," she said, her voice warm as a summer breeze. "The hanged man, which is a hidden influence, simply means you need to put to death outdated ideas or influences or thought patterns and embrace a new, liberating frontier."

One word popped into his mind. He said, "Christianity."

"I'm not surprised," she said. "For centuries we've been persecuted by those of the so-called Christian faith. The tarot is speaking, Philip. You must flee the prison which those ideas hold you in."

Philip's brain was on maximum spin. If true, if Christianity was holding him back, then everything Becka and Scott, and more recently Ryan and Julie, believed was a lie.

"Are you still with me, Philip?"

His eyes flickered. "I'm sorry, yes. It's just . . . just so much to take in all at once."

Madame Theo smiled. "I know, son. We're almost there. The fourth card is what I like to call the counselor, for it is in the position to provide advice," she said. She brought a finger to the side of her head, adding, "You may elect to follow this advice or ignore it at your own peril." She flipped over the card.

A dry swallow and then Philip spoke. "What's . . . uh . . . the old guy with the lantern mean?"

"That's the hermit." Her fingers lingered on the surface of the table.

Philip waited for the implication. "And?"

"The other side is trying to reach you, Philip." Her voice wavered ever so slightly, as if treading on sacred ground. "Hear me, son. You must meditate and open yourself up to the divine spirit guide that's active in the other world."

"Then what?"

She shook her head. "I can't say for sure. Only you can identify the direction in which the streams of life forces move you. But you must listen . . . listen . . . listen."

Philip blinked. Open himself up to what? Or better, listen to whom? And what if he did? What then? Before Philip could answer his own questions, he heard a knock at the door.

Madame Theo looked up, startled. "I'm sorry. This is most unusual." She crossed the room and opened the door.

Philip looked over his shoulder. As far as he could see, it was a delivery service of sorts.

He strained to hear the conversation. The voice on the outside said something about an exception had been made even if she didn't have proper ID for Rita Thomas, whoever that was.

Thirty seconds later, Madame Theo set a white FedEx envelope on the end table next to the incense pot. "Our time is almost gone," she said, quickly returning to her seat. Her mood appeared significantly impatient. "Uh, now where was I?"

Philip raised an eyebrow. "The fifth card, I think."

She exhaled. "Yes. Thank you. I view this as the likely outcome of future events, if you follow the advice provided by the hermit."

"It's a sun," Philip said, noticing a line of perspiration forming across Madame Theo's forehead. "Are you okay?"

She seemed startled by the question. "Yes, fine. Now," she said, fiddling with the edge of her turban, "the sun is a sign that your future . . . will be bright, filled with joy, warmth . . . uh . . . and good things. It's all there for the taking."

"But?"

"But," she said, her eyes darting toward the package and then back to the table. "But . . . you must rely solely on your own energies, insights, and . . . uh, on your inner strength if you are to succeed."

Philip felt a growing sense of uneasiness spread across his chest. Something had put Madame Theo on edge. But what? She seemed fine, until, that is, the package arrived. Why? Why the sudden restlessness?

"There you have it," she said abruptly. "That will be twenty-five dollars."

"Sure thing." Philip reached into his pocket and clutched two bills. "Got change for thirty?"

Madame Theo took the money and then disappeared into the back room. Once she was gone, and in spite of the fact it was none of his business, Philip leaned to his side to inspect the package. Maybe it held a clue that would explain the change in her behavior.

With a squint, he made out the name Rita Thomas on the shipping label. *That's odd,* he thought. *Why did somebody draw a red line through the name and cross it out?*

Beneath the red line, a message had been scrawled: *aka Madame Theo—okay to deliver per district dispatch.*

10

Wednesday
night, a hard, steady rain fell from the darkened sky, accented occasionally by streaks of yellow lightning. Krissi, Ryan, and Becka sat in a booth in the back corner of a local hamburger joint. A handful of stray fries and several crumpled sandwich wrappers stained with special sauce was all that was left on their trays.

Becka drained the last of her chocolate shake. She eyed the clock on the wall: it was almost 8:30 P.M. "Looks like Philip is a total no-show," she said, wiping her hands on a napkin. "What's with that? He knew we were getting together at 6:00 for the movie, right?"

Krissi sighed. She looked away and said, "I guess he completely bailed on me."

"You try his cell phone?" Ryan asked.

"Yeah. I even called and left a message after school reminding him," Krissi said, playing with a burned fry. She tossed it onto the pile. "No answer at his home, either."

"Can you blame him?" Becka asked. "I mean, Scott told me all about what happened at study hall. He's got to be pretty upset."

"Still, he should have called," Krissi said, miffed. She swiped a loose strand of hair from her face. "It kind of makes me mad, you know? I mean, how rude is that for him to just blow me off like this?"

"So," Ryan said after a long moment, "what's with Philip going to see that tarot lady for, anyway?"

Krissi shrugged. "Beats me. I know his dad's been putting tons of pressure on him about college—"

"But . . . a fortune-teller?" Becka interjected. After school, Scott had caught up with her and told her everything—Philip's angry meltdown in the cafeteria, the crazed look in his eyes, and how Scott had never seen Philip so nervous and flipped out.

"Sounds bogus to me, too," Ryan said. "I just don't picture Philip, you know, falling for such a ridiculous—"

Becka jumped in. "Ryan . . ."

He winked. "Okay . . . let's just say, something else must be seriously wrong with him to see, um . . . Madame Whacko."

"Ryan!" Becka said with a punch to his shoulder.

Krissi thought about that for a second. She shifted in her seat. "Well, honestly, maybe he's confused about . . . about us, too. Like, about our future together. I mean, with his dad putting on the pressure for college and all that, maybe he's been afraid of making a commitment."

Becka stole a look at Ryan. She knew the feeling. She had tons of questions about what would happen between her and Ryan. She also knew there were better ways to deal with those concerns than to consult a psychic. The occult was nothing to mess around with. After all that had happened—at the mansion, with Krissi, in the park—surely Philip understood that much, didn't he?

Something else was bothering her about Philip's strange behavior. Z had said that fooling around with tarot cards could be lethal.

Was Philip in danger?

Becka glanced across the table, framing her next question as carefully as she could. "Krissi, you don't think Philip is . . . like . . . suicidal do you?"

Krissi paled. "I . . ."

As if on cue, her cell phone rang. Krissi almost jumped out of her seat. Flustered, she snatched it from her purse, pushed Talk, and said, "It's Krissi."

Krissi noticed Becka watching her as if studying her face to figure out who the caller was.

"Philip!" Krissi said, her eyes darting between Becka and Ryan. "What's going on? Where have you been? We missed you at the movie. I've been so worried—"

Krissi fell silent as she listened, imagining her face morphing into a picture of disbelief, hurt, surprise, and then anger.

"Whatever!" Krissi said a little too loud. She bolted upright and then scrambled out of the booth. She stood, her back to the table, with her right finger pressed against one ear and the phone against the other ear.

"I don't know what's wrong with you. . . ."

"Listen, Krissi, I'm just really confused about so much these days," Philip said.

"As if I hadn't noticed."

Philip cleared his throat. "I . . . I just need some time to sort stuff out."

"Yeah, but what about us? You know, you and me against the world and all that stuff?"

"You know that hasn't changed—"

"Right . . ." Krissi rolled her eyes. "Then why didn't you show tonight? I'm really hurt if you want to know the truth."

Philip remained silent for a moment. "I'm sorry, Krissi. I don't ever want to hurt you, really I don't. But I guess I needed to be alone . . . for a while."

"And meanwhile, what am I supposed to do?"

"Well, I kind of hoped you'd understand my need for some space."

Krissi's voice raised a notch. "Sorry, Philip. I'd like to understand, but I don't. . . ."

"Why not?"

"Just tell me this. How long do I need to stick around to find out if this relationship is going to go somewhere?"

"I don't know," Philip said, his voice growing distant. "And I guess I don't know why you're coming down so hard on me."

"Why? Because you're not the same guy I used to know. . . ."

"How's that?"

"Where's the Philip who used to make me laugh and cry at the same time?"

Philip hesitated. "He's just a little lost right now."

"Still," Krissi said, stealing a look at Ryan and Becka. She lowered her voice. "As far as I'm concerned, our relationship is as good as over!"

Krissi snapped the phone shut and collapsed into her seat.

~

Philip had been driving aimlessly in the rain for hours. He had a vague awareness that it was a little after 8:00 at night. Parked under a railroad bridge, he sat somewhere out in the country away from the problems back in Crescent Bay. His eyes were drained of their tears, his mind was filled with confusion, and his heart was running on empty.

He squeezed the phone against his ear until it hurt. Did Krissi really hang up on him? Was it really over? Numbed that she had, in fact, cut him off, he sat in a daze thicker than the fog blanketing the road ahead. The phone slipped from his hand onto the front seat next to him.

He had just lost his best friend.

The one who stuck by him when his parents were breaking up.

The girl who always seemed to lift his spirits.

The person who seemed to know and care so much about him. A hole formed in the pit of his stomach. Krissi refused to understand—or couldn't understand—his situation. Either way, she was leaving him in the dust.

Maybe breaking up was for the best. Wasn't that what the tarot cards pointed to? According to Madame Theo, Krissi was in the way of his growth, his future fortunes, and his destiny. She was holding back his rising star. Or was she?

Could the cards be wrong?

The more he tossed the situation over in his mind, the more the whole tarot thing seemed so subjective. Even Madame Theo said that he needed to listen to the divine cosmic forces or whatever. Maybe that's where he made a mistake. Maybe he didn't do a very good job of listening. Worse, if he had heard wrong, then he had just played the fool and burned the bridge to the most important friend in his life.

Philip slapped the dash with his right hand.

Several painfully long seconds passed. It seemed to him that the more he struggled to take control of his future, the worse things were starting to become. Fighting back a fresh round of tears, he decided to get home.

Besides, having noticed it was 8:34, if he hurried, he'd be able to catch Madame Theo in her new time slot on TV.

He reached for the keys to start the car. With a whine, the engine conked out. He tried again. Same thing. On the third try, the engine caught. He engaged the transmission, flipped on the wipers, and pulled onto the two-lane road, where he hadn't seen a car in the last thirty minutes.

Philip leaned against his door and drove with one hand draped over the wheel. The wipers flopped from side to side as the lightning flashed across the night sky. He had gone about two miles when the convertible sputtered, stalled, and stopped. The wipers continued their rhythmic thump as he coasted to the curb. Now what? He scanned the gauges and spotted the problem.

He had run out of gas.

Philip pounded the steering wheel with both hands. "Why? . . . Why me? . . . Why now?"

He snapped off the lights, hopped out of the car, and slammed the door so violently the windows shook. He started to wander home in the pouring rain. What choice did he have? He wasn't about to call his dad—or Krissi for that matter.

Within minutes he was soaked through to the skin. His shoes were waterlogged and his hair matted against his forehead until he could have passed for a drenched rat. The deluge of anger surged within him with each step.

Philip lifted his face against the wet blackness and screamed, "God . . . I need answers!"

Nothing but the jagged flash of lightning answered him.

Figures, he thought. Where was God when he needed him? Where was God when his mother decided to split in the middle of the night? Where was God when his dad was bearing down on him? Where? Nowhere, that's where, he decided, shrugging off a chill.

As he strained against the storm, he realized he didn't have the strength to press on. He'd never make it. Furious, Philip kicked the ground, turned, and headed back to the car where he had left the cell phone. Once inside the car, he swallowed his pride, dialed a number, and prayed for a small miracle.

Come on, Scott, answer the phone.

∼

Scott sat at his desk in his bedroom and suppressed a yawn. He stared at the computer screen. He had just finished telling Z about the disaster with Philip at school and was waiting for Z's take on the situation. Z's answer finally appeared.

*Scott, keep in mind, not all tarot readers know
what they're doing. It's a highly subjective field.
Many are simply guessing about possible
outcomes based on what they perceive
the client wants to hear.*

But I thought you said tarot cards were lethal.

*Yes, They can be. Turning to tarot opens
a person up to very real dangers.*

See. So I was right to have warned Philip.

This time, Z answered Scott with a question of his own. The words crawled across the screen:

*Scott, the Bible says unbelievers will know
we are Christians by our what?*

By our love. But that's so unfair, Z. Philip's
fooling around with tarot cards. They're
dangerous. You said so yourself.

*When we are wronged, what does
Jesus want us to do?*

I guess turn the other cheek.

Scott shook his head, upset by the direction of the conversation. After all, Philip was

the one who kicked him out of the car.
Philip was the one who yelled at him in front
of everybody in the cafeteria. Philip was the
one who was being a jerk. Still feeling defensive, he fired off another response:

> Yeah, but, Z, Philip is the one who's gone
> off the deep end. Not me.

Scott waited. After a long pause, Z typed
back:

> *You can be theologically correct about tarot cards,*
> *Scott, and still have no heart in it. Maybe what*
> *Philip sees in you is judgment and condemnation.*

> What am I supposed to do?

> *Just love him.*

> How?

Scott waited for a response, but none
came. That was like Z, too. Half the time it
seemed Z wanted Scott and Becka to figure
things out on their own. Scott yawned,
stretched his arms, then signed off and
folded his arms. This wasn't what he wanted
to hear. Secretly, he had hoped Z would have
at least applauded him for trying his best and
then told him to drop the whole thing. The

clock next to his bed indicated it was 8:44. With another yawn, he shut down the computer.

Scott scratched the back of Cornelius' head for several seconds. It had been one of the longest days of his life, at least emotionally. First, the study hall fiasco. Then the confrontation in the cafeteria, not to mention all the little jabs he had overheard in the hallway throughout the rest of the day.

He covered his mouth as another yawn emerged. He still had a pile of homework to do, but that would have to wait until he grabbed a few minutes of rest. He turned out the lights and then crashed against his pillow. He closed his eyes as the dull patter of rain against the roof serenaded him to sleep.

Within seconds, he heard a window on the other side of the bedroom blow open. He propped himself up on one arm. He quickly scanned the darkness. Against the flash of thunder, he saw a faceless intruder sneaking across the room. It was just steps away, moving in his direction. Scott's heart spiked.

The figure, hunched over and cloaked, made no noise as it drifted like a phantom to the edge of the bed.

"Who's there?" Scott asked, suddenly feeling fully awake.

No answer.

A crack of lightning lit up the intruder's

features. For a split second, Scott caught a glimpse of her face. He knew this woman, but he had no idea why she had trailed him home.

Scott found his voice. With a croak, he said, "What . . . what do you want with me?"

11

Her long, bony forefinger was as thin as a twig. With a jab, she punctured the night air in Scott's direction. A harsh crackle roared in the distance followed by several flashes of light. The drapes by the open window flailed about like two sails in the wind, beating against the mad rush of angry air.

The ghostlike figure leaned over his bed.

Her eyes glowed like two hot charcoals. Her skin, a washed-out mixture of ashen and gray, seemed to hang from her bones. Her breath smelled of rotting garbage, and the wraps of her turban appeared mummylike.

Scott's heart zoomed as his mind raced to find answers. All he managed to say was, "Madame Theo?"

"Silence!" She poked his side with her bony finger.

Scott jumped backward, rubbing the spot she had pierced. It burned as if her finger had been dipped in acid. "What in the world—"

"He's mine . . . all mine."

"Who . . . who is?" Scott asked, still dazed by the encounter.

"Philip." Madame Theo circled the bed, running, floating, flying. With each revolution, she poked Scott again and again, shouting, "Philip . . . Philip . . . Philip . . ."

Try as he did, he was unable to avoid the piercing sting of her fingertip. He felt as punctured as a pincushion. His lungs began to constrict as he tried to catch his breath. Somewhere in the distance, a bell started ringing. The hollow clanging echoed in his head until it throbbed.

Scott tried to sit upright—had to sit up—but Madame Theo knocked him down with a blow to the chest. The force of her hand compressed the remaining air from his burning lungs. He felt a prolonged pressure crushing against his rib cage as if caught in the jaws of a giant invisible vise.

"Stay away from Philip," she bellowed. She reached out and grabbed the corner of the bed. With a jerk, she sent the bed spinning in a circle. Scott held on for dear life.

Like a wounded animal, Madame Theo howled, "He's mine . . . all mine."

Just as quickly as the ordeal had started, it stopped.

The bed came to a rest. Madame Theo was gone.

With the exception of the thunder and the rain pelting the roof, the room was deadly silent. In the thick silence that followed her stormy appearance, the ringing inside of Scott's head grew louder and louder, more intense with each second until he could no longer bear it. Covering his ears with the palms of his hands, Scott yelled, "Stop it!"

With a blink, Scott woke from the nightmare. Drenched in sweat, his heart hammering against his chest, he sat up and tossed his legs over the edge of the bed. The windows were closed. The drapes hung in place.

The phone was ringing.

Scott fumbled in the dark for the portable handset. "Hello?"

"Scott?"

The voice was familiar, but the connection was so bad he didn't recognize it at first. "Yeah?"

"It's Philip."

Scott sat upright, alert. Was this part of the nightmare, too? After all, Philip was the last person he expected to hear from. Scott switched on a lamp. He was awake. This was no dream. "What time is it?"

"Like, 9:45," Philip said. "Sorry. Did I wake you up?"

"I . . . I must have dozed for a minute," Scott said.

As he regained consciousness, Scott was about to give Philip a piece of his mind for yelling at him at school when Z's words—*just love him*—came to mind. Scott blew a short breath. He really wasn't in a mood to be loving. Then again, maybe this was one of those divine appointments Z always talked about.

"Scott?"

"I'm here," Scott said, rubbing the spots where Madame Theo had poked him in his dream.

"I've been trying to get through, but your line was busy."

See, Scott thought, *he's already trying to pick a fight.* Instead of jumping to conclusions, Scott said, "I was on-line. Um, that is, before I fell asleep. So what's up, man?"

"I . . . I could really use your help."

"Mom, can I borrow the car?" Scott asked. Although he had turned sixteen a month ago and had been taking drivers ed, he knew it was a long shot if she agreed. He stood in the doorway to her bedroom where she was reading a book in bed.

"Isn't it kind of late?"

Scott resisted a yawn. "Yeah, but Philip's car broke down. He needs a lift. I figure it's the least I can do for him."

She placed a finger in the page where she had been reading and then partially closed the book. "I don't know. It's raining pretty hard out there—"

"I'll be careful."

She studied his face. "I know you want to help, but can't Philip just call a tow truck?"

"Yeah, he might have been able to, but I think his battery went dead or something," Scott said, leaning against the doorjamb.

"I don't know," she said, placing the book in her lap. "Maybe I should get up and take you."

"I really don't think that'd be too cool," Scott said. "I mean, thanks for the offer and all that, but I think we've got some stuff we need to hash out."

Mrs. Williams nodded. "Okay, son. Just be home by eleven. Remember, better safe than sorry."

Scott kissed her on the forehead, grabbed the keys, and headed for the car.

Scott followed Philip's directions until he spied Philip's car by the side of the road. He pulled alongside of the convertible and, reaching across the seat, Scott unlocked the passenger door.

"Thanks, dude," Philip said, once inside.

"Hey, what are friends for." Scott handed Philip a towel to dry his face and said, "Here, my mom suggested I bring this for you."

"Your mom's cool. Thanks." He started to towel down his hair. "You know, I should have asked you to just bring a gas can. Guess I wasn't thinking."

"Even if you had," Scott said with a smile, "I passed the gas station and it was already closed." He carefully made a U-turn and headed back to town. He considered telling Philip about his bizarre dream with Madame Theo but figured he might just get defensive. "So what happened to the big date? I thought you were going out with Krissi, Ryan, and Becka tonight."

Philip dried the back of his neck. "Honestly?"

Scott tossed him a look. "Sure."

"I'm pretty confused these days, you know?"

Scott thought of a wisecrack but decided against saying it.

"Anyway," Philip said, toweling down his arms, "I just didn't see the point, at least, not after what Madame Theo said today."

At the mention of her name, Scott's heart flinched. "You saw her again?"

Philip cautiously eyed Scott.

"Look, about today . . . I am so sorry, man," Scott said. "I shouldn't have talked about you behind your back. I mean, it's not like I was gossiping. It's just that some of us think you're changing. We care, that's all."

Philip wrapped the towel around his neck. He leaned an elbow against the passenger door. "Can I trust you not to blab?"

Scott nodded. "I promise."

For the next several minutes, Philip told Scott about the five-card spread, Madame Theo's interpretation, and the changes he thought he needed to make—including putting some distance between himself and Krissi. After he was finished, Philip fell silent.

For his part, Scott wanted to warn him about the dangers of getting involved with tarot cards. He couldn't shake the feeling that Philip was walking on very dangerous ground. Instead of giving him a lecture, he tried a different approach.

"You're taking this tarot stuff pretty seriously, huh?" Scott said, stealing a quick look at his passenger.

"I don't know what to think," Philip said. "But—"

"But what?"

"Something happened today that was kind of weird."

Scott raised an eyebrow. "Like, how?"

"She got a package. One of those overnight deals," Philip said, looking out his window. "It came during my session."

"What's so weird about that?"

"I could be wrong, but she started acting really different afterward," Philip said. "It was like she had lost interest in the cards and wanted me to leave."

Scott wrinkled his nose. "I don't get it. What's wrong with that? She probably had stuff to do."

Philip shook his head. "Actually, the weird part had to do with the name on the package."

"How's that?"

"Just that it was addressed to somebody called Rita Thomas."

"So?"

"Well, she's the only one there," Philip said with a shrug. "Maybe it's nothing. But Rita's name was crossed out and it said aka Madame Theo or something like that."

Scott looked at Philip and waited for an explanation. "What's aka mean?" he finally asked.

"That means, also known as," Philip said.

Scott allowed the information to sink in. Then it hit him. "So Madame Theo is *also known as* Rita Thomas."

"I knew there was something going on with her," Philip said.

They rode in silence for half a mile, when Scott asked, "Why the different names?"

"That's what I don't get," Philip said, wiping his face with the towel again. "Why doesn't she just call herself Madame Rita? Unless—"

Scott finished his sentence. "Unless she's hiding something."

"But what's she hiding?"

12

*P*hilip ducked inside the kitchen door, hoping to dash up the back staircase to his room without being detected by his dad. He could tell his dad was still awake by the bluish flicker of light in the den. Philip figured he had probably fallen asleep with the TV on, but he didn't take any chances. He removed his waterlogged sneakers and started for the steps.

A voice from the den called out, "Do you have any idea what time it is?"

Philip swallowed hard. "Just after eleven."

"May I ask where you've been all night?" his dad asked, appearing at the door to the kitchen. A beer dangled from the fingers in his right hand.

"I kind of ran out of gas, sir."

A pained look crossed his father's face. He took a sip from the can. "You what?"

"I ran out—"

"I heard you the first time. Now sit down."

Philip took a seat at the kitchen table. He had an idea of what was coming and desperately wanted to avoid another argument. But how? Once Dad started drinking, it was impossible to have a rational conversation.

"You expect me to believe that story, buddy boy?" his dad said, staggering toward the table. "Well, I don't. I wasn't born yesterday. You were out with that . . . that Missy girl."

"It's Krissi, and no, I wasn't out with her, Dad. Actually, can we talk about this tomorrow?"

His dad waved him off. "How come you're soaking wet?"

"It's raining, remember?"

"Hey, watch it, buster." His dad finished the beer and reached for another from the refrigerator. "I want to talk to you about . . . about your college plans."

Philip shook his head. "Please, Dad, not again. I—"

His dad smacked the table with his palm. "We're done talking when I say we're done. Got it?"

"Dad, cut me some slack here," Philip said, starting to rise. "It's late and I'd like to get some dry clothes on."

"Shut up . . . and sit down."

"Dad, come on," Philip said, moving toward the stairway. "You're drunk. Let's talk in the morning, okay? I promise."

His dad swore and then threw an empty beer can in Philip's direction. It ricocheted off a cabinet and, falling to the floor, flipped several times before coming to a stop. A trickle of beer leaked out. "You're just like your mother . . . always looking for a quick exit. Go on. Get out of here. I can't stop you from ruining your life."

Glad to make his getaway, glad to distance himself from his drunken father, Philip ran up the stairs two steps at a time. He tossed off his wet clothing, dried himself off, and pulled on shorts and a T-shirt. He snapped off the lights and jumped into bed. He exhaled a long, tired breath.

Alone in the darkness, Philip tried to sleep but couldn't stop thinking about Krissi. On the one hand, he was dying to call her, to hear her voice, to know that everything would still work out between them. Maybe if he, like Scott, apologized, they'd get back together.

On the other hand, maybe Madame Theo was right. Maybe Krissi was holding him back. Maybe she wasn't good enough for him and she, like his mother, would dump him when things got tough. Then again, it bothered him that Madame Theo might be hiding something. But what? Was she really who she claimed to be? He had been so quick to believe everything she had been saying. What if she was just another scam artist after a quick buck?

Philip rolled over onto his side and thought about the hunting knife hidden between his mattresses. Why did life have to be so hard? Why was he under such pressure to perform? To please his dad? To get good grades? Why couldn't he get a grip? Would anybody really miss him if he were gone? The more he thought things through, the more depressed he became.

In the darkness he slipped out of bed, sat on the floor, and reached for the knife. He rested the blade across his lap and slumped against the bed. With this final desperate act, he could settle his struggles once and for all.

Death would free him from the heavy burden that had weighed him down for years.

No more encounters with a drunken parent.

No more upset girlfriends.

No more unanswered questions.

No more uncertainty about the future.

Death was the answer. Or was it? His heartbeat quickened.

There was something about the finality of death that scared him. What happened when he died? Did he just cease to exist? Or was there something or someone out there? He couldn't shake the feeling that he wasn't ready to face the great unknown. It was then that a face came to his mind.

Becka.

Of all the people he knew from school, Becka seemed different. There was an irresistible warmth behind her smile. A brightness in her eyes. A self-confidence that didn't appear forced. Sure, she had problems. She made mistakes. But there was something about Becka that he couldn't ignore.

Becka had peace.

That's it, Philip decided. No matter the circumstances, she seemed at peace. And she wasn't afraid to stand for what she believed, even when battling evil spirits. Why? What was it about Becka that gave her the strength to carry on—even after the untimely plane crash involving the dad she loved?

He knew Becka claimed to be a Christian and that she believed in Jesus. But he couldn't figure how that would make any real difference. In fact, Philip remembered a time when he had been curious about Jesus, too. But his interest was sidetracked by other important stuff—like Krissi and school and his car.

Now, hanging on to the end of his rope, there was a part of him wishing he had been as thorough in his investigation of Christianity as he was of Madame Theo's tarot cards. Was it too late to reconsider Jesus?

In the cold, dark shadows of the night, Philip broke into a sweat. His breathing was hard and labored. His head ached as if he'd been clobbered by a baseball bat. More than anything, he wished he had someone to talk to. Someone who might pull him back from the cliff. Someone, anyone, who cared.

God, if you're there . . . I need a sign . . . a friend . . . just something—

Philip hadn't finished his prayer when the phone by his bed purred. His heart leaped. *Probably a wrong number,* he thought. It rang again. And it rang a third time as he reached for the phone. He cleared his throat. "Hello?"

"Dude, it's Scott."

Philip's heart skipped a beat. "Hey, Scott."

"Hope I didn't wake you up. You okay?"

"Sure, why do you ask?"

"I don't know. Just felt this need to call you," Scott said. "I mean, I know this may sound far out—"

"No, go ahead," Philip said, hoping he didn't sound as shocked as he felt.

"Well, ever since I got home, I've had this impression like God wanted me to call." Scott paused.

Philip held the phone between his shoulder and his ear as he studied the knife. "Uh, everything's okay. I'm just kind of burned-out. You know how that goes."

"I do," Scott said. "Hey, I'll be praying for you."

Philip swallowed. "Thanks, Scott."

"By the way, I sent an e-mail to Z tonight and told him about the whole Rita Thomas thing," Scott announced. "Maybe he can dig something up on her. Hope you don't mind. He's amazing. I bet he'll come up with something."

"That's cool," Philip said.

"See you tomorrow?"

"Uh, sure."

~

On Thursday morning Madame Theo sat in the stuffed leather chair facing the desk of

Fred Stoner, her producer. The new time slot worked great. Her guest was wonderful. The phone bank in Utah was swamped with callers looking to get a peek at their future. The money was starting to roll in. The first round of syndication was working. But, at the moment, none of that mattered.

She studied Fred's face like a hawk as he flipped through several documents—secret papers sent to her from Zack Zimmerman, her lawyer in Los Angeles. As far as she could tell, Fred was unmoved by what he saw. He showed about as much emotion as a houseplant. He flipped over another page and, scanning the contents, shook his head.

"This is what you were concerned about?" he said after a prolonged silence.

"Shouldn't I be?" Madame Theo asked, puzzled by his indifference.

"Not in the least," he said, dropping the papers to his desk. "It's old news. I'm no lawyer, but it seems to me that the statute of limitations has run out on these . . . these—"

"Crimes," she said, adjusting her turban. "I'm not proud of what I did, but I'm not offended to use the right term."

"Listen to me," he said, massaging his temples. "That was then. This is now. And you're hot. Do you understand that?"

Madame Theo tried to appear surprised.

"I'm telling you," Fred said, flashing a

mouth full of highly polished teeth, "you're about to step into the big time. I'm talking hyperspace. I'm talking mounds of cash once we ramp up to full syndication. This . . . this stuff is old news. In my view, you don't have anything to lose sleep over."

Madame Theo folded her arms. "Really? You think so?"

"Really." Fred Stoner walked to her side, helped her up, and guided her toward the hall. "It's late. Get some rest. Tomorrow I'll pull out all the stops. We'll go live in Los Angeles. Nothing can go wrong."

"But—"

Fred put an arm around Madame Theo's shoulders. "Trust me. Who's gonna know our little secret, anyway? Right?"

13

Scott raced
through the halls between classes. He had an
idea of where Philip would be—or should be
was more like it. So far, four periods into
Thursday morning and still no sign of Philip
anywhere. None of Philip's friends had spotted him either. Scott was getting anxious
after what had happened last night.

All morning, Scott replayed the phone

conversation from the previous night in his
mind. Something in Philip's voice scared
him. Not in the words spoken. No. There
was just something very dark about his tone.
Philip sounded desperate. Distant.
Depressed. And a bit edgy. But why?

Even though Scott was no expert, Philip's
erratic behavior the last few days struck him
as borderline suicidal. Would Philip take his
own life? Scott refused to think Philip would
do something so drastic. Or would he? Come
to think of it, what was Philip doing way out
on that deserted country road in the middle
of the night?

Scott dashed into the cafeteria and
scanned the mass of faces around the tables.

Off to his left, somebody called his name.
"Hey, Scott, over here."

Scott turned. Krissi, Ryan, and Becka were
sitting together at a table by the far wall. He
waved and then worked his way through the
crowded lunch room.

"What's up, Scott?" Ryan said, studying
Scott's face as he approached. "You look like
someone died."

Scott shot him a look. "That's not funny."

"It was a joke, Scott."

"Whatever." Scott ran his fingers through
his hair. "Listen. Have you guys seen Philip?"

Krissi flushed. Ryan and Becka exchanged
a look.

"What did I say?" Scott said, stealing a fry from Becka's plate.

"It's just that Krissi broke up with Philip last night," Becka said, smacking Scott's hand as he reached for another fry.

"Wow," Scott said. "That's a bummer. Still, did you guys see him today?"

Krissi, her cheeks red as roses, shook her head. "No."

"Me neither," Ryan said, then looked at Becka.

Becka frowned. "No. Is something up?"

Scott's eyes zoomed around the room to see if anybody was eavesdropping. He had learned his lesson during study hall and didn't care to cause more damage. He leaned forward as if revealing a national secret. "Last night, I wanna say around eleven-ish, I had this really strong feeling that I needed to call him. You know, one of those God-prompting things our pastor is always talking about."

"Really?" Becka said, her eyebrows raised. "I had a sense that I should pray for him, too."

"Anyway, I called and he sounded—" Scott paused, unsure whether or not to say something that might make Krissi worry. "He sounded really down."

Krissi folded her arms together. "What makes you say a thing like that?"

"Call it a guy's intuition—"

"There's no such thing," Krissi said with a flick of her hair.

"Still," Scott said, unfazed by her protest, "I think he's into this tarot card craze deeper than even he realizes."

"How's that?" Becka asked, looking worried.

Scott stole another look around. "Just that he's really hung up about what's in the future—you know, like, about college, friends, stuff like that."

Ryan put an arm around Becka. "He's not the only one with those kind of questions," he said. "Take your sister and me. We're wondering what God has for us down the road, too."

Scott's right eyebrow shot up. He nudged Becka with an elbow. "What's this I'm hearing, sis?"

Becka looked away. Her face turned four shades of red.

"Oh, now I get it," Scott said, as if solving a great mystery.

"Get what?" Becka said, guarded.

"Well, if things are cruising between you two," Scott said with a wink, "that explains why you were singing happy songs while washing the dishes."

Becka nailed him in the shoulder with a fist. "SCOTT! You are *so* clueless."

"The point is," Ryan said, rescuing Becka from further embarrassment, "we've been studying what the Bible says about our future, you know, next year with college and all of that."

"And?" Scott asked, checking his sister's reaction.

"That's the interesting part," Becka said. "There's a verse in Zechariah—"

"It's chapter 10 verse 2," Ryan said, nodding.

"Ooh, bonus points." Scott laughed.

"ANYWAY," Becka said, rolling her eyes, "it says, 'Household gods give false advice, fortune-tellers predict only lies, and interpreters of dreams pronounce comfortless falsehoods.' "

"Which means?" Krissi asked.

Ryan stretched. "Well, it definitely means using stuff like tarot cards is out of the question."

Becka added, "We don't know exactly what God has in mind. What we do know is that, in Jeremiah 29:11, God says, 'I know the plans I have for you. . . . They are plans for good and not for disaster, to give you a future and a hope.' "

"That's why it doesn't make sense to mess around with fortune-tellers," Ryan said. "God's already promised to take good care of us."

Krissi shrugged. "I guess I see your point—"

"Hey, that reminds me," Ryan said. "Didn't Pastor Todd do something on fortune-tellers and those two dudes, Paul and Stylus?"

Scott laughed. "I think you mean Paul and *Silas*. And you're right. Pastor Todd covered that in a study on the book of Acts."

"Right."

Scott grabbed several fries from Becka's plate. He popped them in his mouth and started to talk. "Well . . . those guys—"

"Paul and Silas," Ryan interjected.

"Yeah, them," Scott said with a nod. "They were on a missionary trip somewhere and this fortune-teller girl was following them around being a real pain. So one day, Paul turned around and cast the demon out of her. Which, naturally, ticked off the guys who were making big bucks with her."

Becka smiled. "Looks like you actually stayed awake at least once during youth group."

Scott's eyes narrowed. "Nice. Don't you see? Her fortune-telling was connected to demon possession."

Krissi gasped at the implication. "Are you saying that . . . that Madame Theo is, like, possessed?"

Scott threw up both hands. "Hey, not necessarily. And I don't claim to know that about her for sure. I'm not even saying demon possession is always going on with tarot-card readers. I'm just saying that Philip is getting mixed up in some dangerous stuff. Even Z said that tarot cards are lethal."

No one spoke for a long minute. A food fight broke out at the next table, and Scott tossed a fry in their direction just for fun. He turned and faced Ryan, Becka, and Krissi. He wanted to tell them about the whole Rita Thomas mystery, too, but he had promised Philip he'd keep his mouth shut. If only Z had answered his e-mail about Rita's identity from last night.

For no apparent reason, Becka jumped. She reached into her pocket and pulled out her phone. "Sorry! I set my cell phone on vibrate and I'm not used to it." She flipped it open and brought it to an ear. "Hello?"

Scott watched Becka's face as she listened. "It's for you, Scott," she said, handing him the phone. She eyed him suspiciously. "Is this some kind of prank?"

Scott gave her a puzzled look. "Why do you ask?"

Becka, obviously flustered as if she had eaten a piece of raw squid, blinked twice. "The guy says he's Z."

Scott had difficulty finding his voice. A thousand questions flooded into his mind. Could this really be Z? How could he know for sure? What if this was, like Becka said, just an elaborate prank? As long as they had been communicating, Z never used the phone—they only connected by e-mail or instant message. Why would he call this time?

He raised the phone to his ear and tried to speak. "Z?"

"Good afternoon, Scott," the voice said.

Whoever was calling somehow modified his voice, of that Scott was sure. He was also fairly certain of something else. Z was a man. But who?

"I . . . Z? Is that really you?"

"I got your e-mail, Scott. From last night."

Scott swallowed. The back of his throat burned. *It must be Z,* he thought. Who else knew about the e-mail besides himself and Philip? Could it be Philip just messing with his mind? Scott had to be sure. He had to think of something that only he and Z would know. But what? The food fight at the next table was getting out of hand, and Scott was having trouble thinking on his feet.

"Um, Z . . . I . . . I—"

"You're having doubts it's me, right?"

"You can say that again."

"Then ask me a question."

"Um, okay. What did you write . . . in your last e-mail?"

"I told you a friend was in danger and desperately needs your help. I sent it along with the video file of Madame Theo's TV show."

"It *is* Z!" Scott said to Becka, exchanging a quick, wide-eyed look with his sister. He got up, walked closer to the window and away from the commotion brewing behind him.

"I don't have much time. This is very important."

Scott covered his other ear with a hand. He hoped the pounding of his heart wouldn't drown out the conversation. "Go ahead. I'm listening, Z."

"You asked about Rita Thomas."

"Right."

"Your instincts were correct. Rita Thomas and Madame Theo are one and the same person."

Scott couldn't believe he was actually talking to Z. He tried to remain focused. He closed his eyes to block out all distractions. "And?"

"My sources—which I cannot reveal, so don't ask—informed me thirty years ago, Madame Theo, whose real name is Rita Thomas, lived in Los Angeles. Rita read palms and tarot cards on a local cable channel. She had a toll-free number. Business was good. Too good. The police were called in to investigate thousands of complaints to the phone company about excessive charges. Her people were running a scam on the public that ran into millions of dollars."

Scott let out a low whistle.

"A grand jury found enough evidence to believe she was guilty of violating the RICO statutes."

"RICO?"

"That's an abbreviation for Racketeering Influenced and Corrupt Organizations Act."

"Never heard of it," Scott said, feeling over-whelmed by both the fact he was talking to Z and that Z had somehow unearthed this information.

"Scott, the government uses that law to bust people who are involved with organized crime. Rita Thomas, it turns out, was in pretty deep, too."

Scott felt chilled. What was Philip getting into?

"But there's more," Z said, his hollow voice echoing through the distortion device. "Rita Thomas had one of the best defense lawyers in the country, a Zack Zimmerman, who has himself proved to be a shady character."

"Should I be taking notes?" Scott asked, his heart pounding.

"No. Just listen." Z paused. "I don't have much more time. The case went to trial, and Zack and his team of crackpot lawyers lost. Everything Rita owned was confiscated. She was ordered to repay millions of dollars. She also faced serious jail time."

"I don't get it," Scott said, trying to connect the dots. "How is she still in business—right here in Crescent Bay?"

"To avoid jail, Rita faked her death in a fiery car crash. I say faked because, while it was her Mercedes they found burned at the bottom of a cliff in Malibu, the detectives could never properly identify the body as being hers. My best guess is that she moved north to Crescent Bay, changed her name, and started over."

"And since it's been so many years ago, she figures nobody will remember, right?" Scott asked.

No answer. Scott looked at the phone and saw they were still connected. "Hello? Z? You still there?"

"Scott, I'm still here, but I must go."

"What about Philip? What should I—"

"Madame Theo's a dangerous person who will stop at nothing, Scott. Don't be fooled by her looks. If Philip lets on that he noticed a connection between Rita Thomas and Madame Theo, he could be in real trouble."

Scott's heart was pounding so hard, it tested the limits of his rib cage.

Z said, "Thanks to this tip, the local police working with the FBI, who get involved in RICO cases, are headed to arrest Madame Theo later today. But you must find Philip. Warn him about the dangers. And, Scott—"

"What's that?"

"When this is over, remember . . . just love him."

"Who?" Scott asked. "Who, Z?"

"Philip. Good to talk with you. Z out."

"Don't go . . . Z . . ."

The connection was terminated. Although disappointed, a new thought struck him like a bolt of lightning. Working quickly, Scott followed the menu prompts that led to the Incoming Call History. Maybe, just maybe, he could tell Z's number. That way, they'd be able to call him back or at least know what area code the mysterious Z had called from.

The call display read: *Unknown.*

14

For Scott, the rest of the afternoon was a complete blur. He had a million questions, not the least of which was how did Z know Becka had a cell phone? How did he know her number? What's more, how did Z know they were together at lunch? A lucky guess? Or was Z somewhere in the building?

Sitting in last period, ignoring his biology

teacher as she droned on and on about some insect body part, Scott eyed the clock mounted above the classroom door. The second hand moved slower around the face of the clock with each minute, as if it were out of breath, too tired to make another revolution.

Scott sighed. His mind drifted back to his conversation with the elusive Z. He was stunned at how Z was able to dig up so much stuff on Madame Theo so quickly. The guy must have amazing connections, Scott decided. Maybe he was in the CIA or the FBI or some top secret branch of government that nobody knew about. If only he had had a few more minutes to talk with Z.

More than anything, Scott was worried about Philip. Where was he? Didn't he say he'd be at school? How could he warn Philip about Madame Theo if he couldn't find him? And what would happen if he was too late?

The bell sounded. Scott dashed out of his seat like a horse on a racetrack and headed for the door. At Becka's suggestion, he kept the cell phone just in case Z called again. Once outside, Scott dialed Philip's cell. He had tried several times already between classes with no success. He figured it was worth one more try.

On the second ring, Philip answered. "Hello?"

The connection was filled with static. "Philip, it's me, Scott. Where have you been, man? You okay?"

"Hey, Scott. It's a long story. My dad woke up with a mean hangover. It didn't help when I told him I had run out of gas. He really blew a gasket, you know?"

"I bet."

"Yeah, so get this. He gives me the gas can—the one we use for the lawn mower—anyway, he drops me off with it in the middle of the highway and tells me to walk the rest of the way."

Scott pictured Philip walking for miles out to the country. No wonder he was gone all day.

"Hey, my battery is about to run out," Philip said. "Guess I left the phone on in the car all night after you picked me up—"

Scott started to panic. He had to tell him about Z's warning. "Listen, Philip, whatever you do—"

"Scott, you're breaking up. I don't know if you can hear me, but there's something I have to do before—"

"Philip—wait! Whatever you do, don't go to Madame Theo's—"

More static.

"Yes, you're right, I have to go to Madame Theo's . . . hello? Scott? You still there?"

"Philip . . . I said, DON'T go to Madame Theo's—"

"My battery is flashing," Philip said. "I got to know if—"

"Listen to me," Scott said desperately. "I talked to Z. Madame Theo *is* Rita Thomas. She's running a scam or worse. She lived in Los Angeles and faked her death to avoid going to jail. Z said she's dangerous . . . did you hear me, Philip?"

Static filled Scott's earpiece and then nothing. Scott's heart sank. He looked at the digital display. It flashed two words: *Connection lost.*

"What's wrong?" Becka asked, appearing at Scott's side.

"I was trying to warn Philip about Madame Theo, but his battery died."

Becka offered a smile. "At least he's okay, right?"

Scott put the phone away. "Yeah, but who knows for how long?"

"Why's that?"

"Philip said he was going to Madame Theo's!"

~

"Yes, please come in," Madame Theo said, waving Philip toward the table. "I'm glad I had an opening this afternoon for my special friend."

Philip stepped into the candlelit room and took his usual seat without saying a word.

"You're troubled, my son." Madame Theo adjusted her turban and then placed her hands palms down on the table. "What is the source of this bad karma?"

Philip tilted his head. He knew this wasn't going to be easy. He wasn't sure why he was even bothering. After all, it wasn't like he cared anymore. Even before he had heard the last part of Scott's message, he had decided to confront Madame Theo with a few things—like her real identity.

Although he couldn't respond because his battery had run out, he was amazed to know Z had said she was running a scam. What kind of scam? From what he could tell, Madame Theo appeared genuine. She seemed somehow connected to the messages in the cards. Could she fake that, too?

"I . . . I have so many questions," Philip began.

"Yes, Philip. That's understandable. That's why the tarot is such a gift."

Philip studied her face. She seemed so sincere. No way could she be mixed up in something illegal. Could she?

"Tell me, Philip, what is weighing on your heart?" She closed her eyes in anticipation of his response as she had done in the past.

Philip cleared his throat. "Actually, I'm

wondering if you could clear something up—
something that's been bothering me ever
since, well, since you got that package yesterday."

Madame Theo's eyes blinked open. "What
package?"

"Remember the one that came from
FedEx? It was delivered in the middle of our
session."

"That is no concern of yours." Her stiff
tone surprised him.

"Well, in a way it is," Philip stammered,
aware that she was growing defensive. He felt
a bead of sweat form on his forehead. "I
mean, you know everything about me. I figure it's only fair if I know the truth about
you."

Madame Theo's stare intensified. She
remained as frozen in place as a statue.

Philip was finding it difficult to breath.
"I . . . I couldn't help but notice it was
addressed to Rita Thomas, but it also said aka
Madame Theo. So which is it?"

"What do you think you know, son?"
Madame Theo said, her voice deepening.
Gone was the warm, grandmotherly tone.

Maybe it was the incense. Maybe it was the
fact that he had walked more miles than he
could count that morning to get to his car.
Maybe it was the lack of lunch. Maybe it was
the anger he detected behind her eyes.

Whatever the reason, Philip was growing dizzy.

Light-headed, Philip felt as though the room tilted one direction, and then, just as quickly, it tilted to the opposite angle. Philip fought with his senses to gain some level of control.

"I just need to know if you're, you know, the real thing," he managed to say, forcing a smile.

"What are you talking about?"

"Please just tell me this. Did you live in Los Angeles?"

No answer. But her nose flared as if she were a provoked bull ready to stampede.

Philip figured he might as well go for broke. He had no idea what he was walking into. He didn't even have all the facts because he wasn't the one who had talked with Z. His curiosity got the better of him. He blurted, "Just tell me that you're not the same Rita Thomas who faked her death, are you?"

"How dare you accuse me of such things," she bellowed in a voice that was no longer her own. Her face twisted and snarled into a knot of rage. She rose to her feet and raised both arms as if calling upon unseen forces.

Behind him, Philip heard a noise. His neck snapped around to see what was happening. The curtains that had covered the windows began to flap as if caught in a violent storm. He turned back to face Madame Theo.

"Who are you to question my powers?" The card table between them suddenly defied gravity. It hovered three feet off the ground, knocking the cards to the floor.

At first, Philip was too stunned to react. His heart pounded for all it was worth. "I . . . it was just a question—"

"Silence, foolish one."

Like a pinball, the table bounced off the walls and headed directly toward him. He fell backward in his chair to avoid contact, hitting the floor with a thud instead.

"You cannot stop us!" the thing inside Madame Theo shouted.

Seconds later, Philip stumbled to his feet when, from across the room, the table swooped down on him like a bat, smashing him in the chest. He slammed against the wall with enough force to drive out the air from his lungs. He blacked out.

~

"Can't this thing go any faster?" Scott shouted.

"Hang on!" Becka pulled their mom's car into the passing lane. "We're almost there!"

"Something's wrong with Philip. I just know it," Scott said, cracking his knuckles.

Becka turned down the street where

Madame Theo's Palace was located.
"There . . . on the right," Scott said with a
point. "That's Philip's car. Hurry!"

∼

Philip lay motionless on the floor. Where was
he? How long had he been here? Why did
everything hurt? A sharp pain seared his
chest. A broken rib? Why was a table jammed
against his chest? And why did it feel as if the
table was still being driven into his body,
crushing him?

His lungs burned. His head throbbed. He
had no strength. His eyes cracked open and
the room spun. He closed his eyes for a second before trying to open them again. It was
then that he saw the flames of a fallen candle
smoldering on the carpet, burning a path
toward him. He tried to move and winced.

"I do not answer to you!" the unearthly
voice said. Although her lips didn't move, it
was Madame Theo talking as she towered
over him. She held a candle dripping with
hot wax over his limp body. "You will learn
what happens to those who doubt."

15

*S*cott jumped
out of the car before Becka had brought it to
a complete stop. He bounded down the side-
walk as fast as his legs could carry him. If Z
said Madame Theo might be dangerous,
then Scott wasn't about to take any chances.
As he approached the storefront, Scott felt
a distinct heaviness of spirit weigh down on

him. A voice in the back of his mind urged him to pray.

Becka raced to his side. "What's wrong?"

"Don't you feel it?" Scott asked.

"Now that you mention it, I do," she said. "Are you thinking what I'm thinking?"

Scott nodded. "Better pray."

"Jesus," Becka said, grabbing Scott's hand, "we've faced the evil one many times before. We know that greater is he who is in us than he who is in the world—"

"Or he who is in Madame Theo," Scott added.

"We bind the power of Satan in this place, in the name of Jesus, amen," Becka said.

Scott squeezed her hand and then pushed open the door to Madame Theo's Palace. With a whoosh the air inside seemed to fight against their entry. Once inside, they were met by a whirlwind of drapes and a blast of pungent air. Scott's eyes burned from the acidic stench of something smoldering. He coughed and, gagging, tried to breathe.

"Over there!" Becka said, coughing. She pointed to the far corner of the darkened room.

The tall, thin figure of Madame Theo was hunched over Philip, holding a candle in her hand. She turned and faced the intruders. "Get back!" she yelled in an agonizing voice not her own. Her eyes blazed. "He's mine . . .

he's mine . . . he's all mine. This is my domain!"

For an instant, Scott flashed back to the nightmare—the one with Madame Theo circling his bed, jabbing him with her finger—but he pushed away the distraction. He stepped forward and said, "You're a liar, Madame Theo! Philip is NOT yours."

With a screech, she tossed the candle toward Philip and raised her hands like a caged animal ready to pounce. The candle ignited the carpet where it fell. The flames ignited the floor, devouring the distance between itself and Philip.

Madame Theo clapped her hands together and the flames, like tongues of fire, started to swirl through the room, slowly at first and then faster and faster, creating a fiery wind tunnel that kindled fires throughout the room. The drapes on the windows. The curtains hanging from the ceiling. The coverings on the walls. All became inflamed in a ghastly chorus of fire.

Scott knew if they didn't act fast, they'd be consumed by the inferno. He took a deep breath and shouted, "By the name above all names, Jesus the Christ, I rebuke you!"

Madame Theo shrieked and staggered backward.

Becka stepped forward to join Scott. "We bind you, spirit of darkness."

"I will not be silenced," the demon squealed.

Scott held out a hand and the beastly thing stuttered. "I order you, father of lies, in the name of Jesus, begone!"

Madame Theo collapsed to the floor, screeching with a rage almost as hot as the flames around them.

"Now!" Becka commanded.

Madame Theo went silent. The wind in the room came to a rest. In the distance, Scott heard the rapid advance of sirens. He cut a path through the flames to Philip's side. "Becka, here, give me a hand . . . hurry!"

Scott looked at Philip's reddened face. His eyes were closed. His breath was labored. With care, but working as fast as he could, Scott pulled the table off Philip. Philip moaned.

"Easy does it, Philip," Becka said. "Just hang on! Help is on the way."

Philip coughed up a mixture of phlegm and blood.

"We've got to get him outside," Scott said, stomping out the fire with his sneakers as the flames licked at Philip's legs. They traded positions. Working together, with Becka now at his feet and Scott at his chest, they carried Philip outside and rested him on a grassy knoll under a tall oak tree.

Scott sat at his computer, exhausted. Although Becka was already fast asleep after the events of the day, it was just nine o'clock. Scott figured he'd give Z an update, that is, if Z was on-line. He typed in his password and paused for the appropriate greeting.

As he waited, his thoughts drifted to Philip, who had been rushed to the hospital where he was being treated for three broken ribs, smoke inhalation, and minor cuts and burns. He thought of Madame Theo, too, who had been handcuffed and arrested by two FBI agents as she tried to slip out the back door of her store.

"Welcome, you've got mail," the computer voice announced.

Scott wasn't interested. Instead, he headed for the chat room where he and Becka had first met Z. He typed a message:

> Z, it's Scott. Are you on-line?

The cursor blinked a dozen times before an answer appeared.

> *Great job today, Scott. How's Philip?*

Scott felt the hairs on the back of his neck tingle. How did Z already know how the day

went? Scott smiled, amazed at the ever mysterious Z.

> I actually got to talk with him for a few
> minutes. He's gonna make it okay. But you
> know what? Philip said he wants to give
> Christianity another try!

> *Very good. I suggest you get him* The Case for
> Christ. *It's a book by Lee Strobel.*

Thanks. He's got plenty of time to read these days!

Scott scribbled the name of the book onto
a scrap of paper. He'd get it for Philip after
school tomorrow. Scott was about to type a
question when more words appeared.

> *Scott, your parents are proud.*

For a second, Scott was puzzled by the
statement. Z knew about his family and how
they had moved to Crescent Bay after his
father's plane crash. They had talked about it
dozens of times. Maybe Z forgot. Scott typed:

> My dad's dead, remember?

Scott stretched and yawned while he
waited for a reply. He cracked his knuckles.
After a minute, he scratched the back of his

head, wondering what was taking Z so long to respond. It was, after all, a simple question.

At long last, Z typed two words:

Is he?

Author's Note

As I developed this series, I had two equal and opposing concerns. First, I didn't want the reader to be too frightened of the devil. Compared to Jesus Christ, Satan is a wimp. The two aren't even in the same league. Although the supernatural evil in these books is based on a certain amount of fact, it's important to understand the awesome protection Jesus Christ offers to those who have committed their lives to him.

This brings me to my second and somewhat opposing concern: Although the powers of darkness are nothing compared to the power of Jesus Christ and the authority he has given his followers, spiritual warfare is not something we casually stroll into. The situations in these novels are extreme to create suspense and drama. But if you should find yourself involved in something even vaguely similar, don't confront it alone. Find an older, more mature Christian (such as a parent, pastor, or youth leader) to talk to. Let him or her check the situation out to see what's happening. Ask him or her to help you deal with it.

Yes, we have the victory through Christ. But we should never send in inexperienced soldiers to fight the battle.

Oh, and one final note. When this series

was conceived, there were really no bad guys on the Internet. Unfortunately that has changed. Today there are plenty of people out there trying to draw young folks into dangerous situations through it. Although the characters in this series trust Z, if you should run into a similar situation, be smart. Anyone can *sound* kind and understanding, but their intentions may be entirely different. All that to say, don't take candy from strangers you see . . . or trust those you don't.

Bill

COOL 2 READ .com
WheRe AdvEnture beGins with a BoOk!
LoG oN @ Cool2Read.com